Isabella L

Pot

History of a journey to the south of the world

Title | Potosi: history of a journey to the south of the world
Author | Isabella Lorusso

ISBN | 978-88-27853-02-3

Cover photo: Mariela Canchari - Peru'© by Macan's photos- All rights reserved.

A special thank to Andrew Hillyard, who corrected the text, and to Valentina Legnani of Traduzioni.eu, the official translator of this book.

© All rights reserved by the Author
No part of this book may
be reproduced without the
prior permission of the Author.

Youcanprint Self-Publishing
Via Marco Biagi 6, 73100 Lecce
www.youcanprint.it
info@youcanprint.it

To Maca'n

And those who were seen dancing
were thought to be insane by those
who could not hear the music.

F. Nietzsche

Isa is bare flesh and yet epidermic and alive

Isabella Lorusso, 19 February 2014
Paola, my dear, how are you? I'm sending you this little work of mine. It's about my life, my childhood, my love affair in Barcelona and my journeys to Latin America. [...] Dreams are dimensions where there's no logic, only love. I'd be so glad if you could take a look at it and write a brief introduction. I don't want to influence you: just trust your heart. Maca'n and I would be very pleased.

Paola Di Matteo, 19 February 2014
I'm fine, thank you. In your 'little work' there is your world, beautiful and embraceable, a world of dreams. I am pleased to read it, but at the same time, I fear that I won't meet your expectations. I'm printing it tomorrow and I'll read it in one go with the wonderful sensation of having you here next to me. If you don't like it, please tell me right away, I already feel so close to your soul. I won't be offended. Please, be honest, as if you didn't know me. The way we recognise each other is weird, isn't it? I feel like I've always had you in my heart, my precious "soul sister." After all, it's not that weird to recognise each other from small things, luckily. By reading your work, I know that I will read about you and Marie, as happened with Otokongo. *I would have stayed with you in that big house, inside pain and beauty, in those eighteen and two hundred*

hours. Smoking, laughing and covering ourselves up in the mud.

Today

I've printed the file that Isabella sent me and I've read Potosì. I could almost open one door in the sky, one in hell and one in a well.
I have 'seen' all the dimensions: body, mind, soul, senses, which make a person one whole entity. Eight, nine, one hundred! Endless doors. It was not actually me opening them; Isabella tore them down to prevent the wind from slamming them down. She did it for us.
That's how this journey began. Isabella and Mariè, all gloriously grimy, went through it with their eyes, tennis shoes, backpacks and life. I've turned this journey into my personal experience and breathlessly clung onto it. I followed the magic circle that starts in via Trinchese, 13 (grandma's white house in Ostuni, Puglia) and ends in Lisbon and Sarajevo, through all the world's meridians and breath. Then, that boundless circle ends up where it began, in Puglia, as all circles close up only to open other infinite ones.
You have promised me you'll let your skin grow. Just a thin, delicate layer of skin over all the things that you have seen, lived and never forgotten.

From Mirò to the prisoners of Lima and the exciting meetings with immense souls.
Huge houses to be shared with stranger friends, a passionate and unforgettable giving and receiving.
Utopias turn into reality with you, Isabella.
What about Andreu Nin[1] *in Moscow? And what about Bolivia and your fierce willingness 'to find El Che*[2]*'? And all the people tortured to death by Fujimori*[3]*? Of course, your skin peels away as your soul opens up to the world, totally defencelessly exposed to it.*
I'm sure that you are eating the black spots on bananas as well. You know, I think about it. I do the same. It will certainly mean something. You are heading back to Europe now, but return journeys are just like the outward ones.
It is just the same: luggage overflowing with skies, that middle space between two stars. Clear light, blue and black. Spices and precious acquaintances. New eyes where constellations shine brightly. No more skin. I finally apologise to you all. I am perfectly aware of the fact that somewhere, inside me, there are some words suitable for a

---

1Andreu Nin i Pérez (El Vendrell, 4 February 1892 – Madrid, 20 June 1937) was a Spanish politician and anti-fascist activist.

2Ernesto Guevara, known as 'El Che' (Rosario, 14 June 1928 – La Higuera, 9 October 1967) was an Argentinian rebel, guerrilla, writer and doctor.

3Alberto Kenya Fujimori (Lima, 28 July 1938) is a Japanese born Peruvian politician, agronomist, physician and mathematician. He was President of Peru from 28 July 1990 to 17 November 2000. He established an authoritarian government, especially after the 1992 self-inflicted coup when all the democratic freedoms were denied.

journey like this. But I am skinless myself and unwilling to describe the world that Isa opens from 'the inside'. Everybody has their own emotions. And they won't be bad.

Thank you very much, Isa.

Paola di Matteo
Poetess and art critic

He paseado por tu jardín agarrada de tu mano,
mientras las últimas hojas otoñales
nos rozaban los abrigos y una
fina lluvia humedecía
nuestros rizos

Preface

Writing a book is like taking a picture. Emotions or situations can change in the blinking of an eye, and yet they have to be described as they were experienced as soon as they are caught. This book deals with some situations which affected a concrete moment of my life. Then my life went on, together with the situations that I have described, but I'm happy I have entered this labyrinth of emotions not to stop them, but rather to break the chains and set them free.

I left from Ostuni, my white city, and landed in Barcelona, the city of Mirò and Gaudì. Then I travelled to Latin America where I met the MRTA and Sendero Luminoso guerrillas in the high-security prisons in Lima. I followed the footsteps of El Che in the Bolivian forest and I worked as a professor at the La Cantuta university for several years, where nine students and a professor were cruelly kidnapped, tortured and killed by Alberto Fujimori's death squads. After many years, I came back to Europe, to Moscow, where I learnt about Andreu Nin, leader of POUM[4], and victim of the Stalinist barbarity. From the Kremlin I moved to the Commerce Square in Lisbon and to the public library in Sarajevo, until I came back to

4 Workers' Party of Marxist Unification

Puglia, to Ceglie, where Maca'n and I fell in love with a tiny white house in the old square of the city.

This book is a journey through several dimensions: the personal and the political one, as well as the relations between women, mothers and daughters. I mean that we can travel all around the world to change it, but first we need to start from ourselves and change what surrounds us, otherwise our efforts will be in vain. I've crossed the ocean, but what I've always dreamt of is a tiny white house by the sea close to my birthplace. Now I have it and I'm so happy that I can leave it once again, because I know where my roots are and they will be the starting point for anything that may follow. I would like to thank all those who have supported me throughout this project as well as those who hindered me, because I've learned that everyone is important but no one is indispensable. Even the woman who gave birth to you can be symbolically replaced by another one. It may take you some years, a lot of efforts, strength and fortune, but even the most unconquerable mountains can be climbed. Finally, I would like to thank Maca'n once again for having been by my side throughout all these years, believing in me and fighting day by day with me, to win a battle which seemed already lost. Our house is a symbol of the rebellion of two women against a hostile world and nobody can take it away from us. We need laws to protect us. I really hope this book will also serve this purpose.

POTOSÌ

History of a journey to the south of the world

I. Moscow

As I was walking along the streets in Moscow, I was thinking about all the years spent in Latin America. I wondered what urged me to go over there and what made me come back to my original place many years later.

I was recalling all my journeys to Patagonia, the people's faces and the smile in a child's eyes. I remembered the first night in Lima in the district where, some years earlier, a Sendero bomb had shocked the city. I was staying at my colleague's house who talked about the lectures that we were going to hold at University. He used to work in Huacho and I was heading northwards, close to the Equator. I would listen to him intrigued.

«The place you are going to,» he said "features a Nature Reserve with crocodiles; rent a boat, go to the isles, have a swim and come back home. It will cost you eight, ten euro, including the crocodile watching.»

Crocodiles? That was the place where I was going to hold my literature lectures and talk about Moravia, Svevo and Carducci? Were my students coming to my lesson on small boats? What were they going to wear? My idea of Peru was very vague. I used to believe that Lima was on the Andes, that people wore straw skirts, went hunting with arrows and lived in trees. I was not that wrong, after all: Peru is four times larger than Italy and has a

considerably low population density with its twenty-eight million inhabitants. Nature embraces you like an octopus and imagination gallops far beyond human limits.
My colleague's wife wanted to come back to Italy. «I can't take it anymore,» she said «A daughter, only few friends and a strong machismo everywhere.» What a good start, I thought.
«Public education doesn't work, you'd better stay away from hospitals, the minimum wage is barely enough to buy cigarettes. Too many social injustices, social differences, and indifferent, complicit and parasitic political classes.»
A part of me was already longing to come back to Italy. I was almost thirty-five years old, most of my friends had already bought houses and settled down. My future there was going to be even more uncertain than the one that I was leaving behind and yet I wanted to experience what could change my life for good.
After all, some people attend master's degrees, others specialise, set up businesses and get rich. Some others have always led uncertain lives and look for stability: they participate in contests, win them and get married. I just wanted to elevate myself, row upstream, learn where the Andes were, talk to the homeless children, not caring about what people said. If the south of the world was hell, that was where I wanted to go.

II. In Latin America. In Lima

As soon as I arrived in Lima, I went to greet the director of the Institute of Italian Culture who had contacted me. I enthusiastically talked to him about my work and he looked at me in astonishment, as if I were a sort of endangered animal. He looked like a very sad man and I felt like hugging him. He said: «Good luck,» but he clearly had something else on his mind. Most of the European officers working abroad earn very high salaries. «That's why he looks so sad,» I thought. How is it possible to live in such a place and not feel like an accomplice of all that misery?

There are about ten million people living in Lima, most of whom were former farmers descended to the valley after a twenty-year civil war between the State and groups of guerrillas, including the Maoist inspired Sendero and MRTA (Tupac-Amaru Revolutionary Movement.) A war which resulted in sixty-nine thousand victims and *desaparecidos* between the Eighties and the year two thousand. It was even worse than Chile and Argentina, in terms of numbers of the victims. Europeans are mostly aware of the massacres of Santiago and Buenos Aires, since the State has wiped out the middle class, and the middle class is important, everybody knows it. According to the Truth Commission, most of the victims in Peru were farmers whose mother tongue was not even Spanish, but Quechua or Aymara. They were the members of the lowest class, recruited by the State and armed by military and paramilitary groups.

The most famous death squad was called Gruppo Colina, named after a murdered policeman. It was established and directed during the dictatorship of Alberto Fujimori, by Martin Rivas and Vladimiro Montesinos, officers of the SIN, the National Intelligence Service. The Gruppo Colina was crueller than the terrorist groups that it claimed to oppose, and specialised in killing and torturing students, trade unionists, academics and regime opponents. They used to cover themselves with hoods and acted in the name of the State.

I used to think about that when I looked at the people's faces; all those beautiful sun-kissed peasant wrinkles. Many homeless children lived on the streets and nobody ever asked them if they wanted an ice-cream, a sandwich or, simply, a caress. Buses pass by and you can grasp the smog exiting from mufflers; car drivers try to run over you, as soon as you cross the street. You don't know who to contact in case of need as policemen are lacking and, on top of that, underpaid. Doctors are always on strike. University lecturers are not even paid in spite of the national agreement.

So, I left Lima and headed northwards to eat fish, talk about Moravia and visit the fascinating Nature Reserve full of crocodiles.

III. Zorritos

Fiorina Sanguinetti, head of the Italian courses at the University, once told me: «If you feel right here, we'll try to make you stay here for a long time.»

I felt pleased at first, but then, when I arrived in the northernmost city in the country, I thought: «*I won't stay here, not even for half a day.*» After having travelled along hundreds of kilometres of desert beaches scattered with palm trees, I arrived in the most desolate place of Latin America, in the middle of nowhere, eighteen hours away from Lima. One square, five trees, four tourists and millions of mosquitoes like vampires. I was a few steps away from the Equator, with a temperature of forty degrees even in winter and that tarmac on streets which seemed to burn inside me. From eleven in the morning to four in the afternoon I could hardly breathe. It was a hell on Earth.

Jorge Echevarría, Dean of the chemistry faculty, drove me to the hotel. I wanted to start the Italian courses at the University right away, but the keyword was: relax, relax and relax. Jorge used to come to me every day and we would have lunch together. At first, I thought that he was kind, but then I found out that the University granted me the refund of the expenses. I could eat free of charge and he was taking advantage of it.

The starting of the courses was delayed and my salary was deferred as well. Fortunately, I received fundings from the Ministry of Foreign Affairs. I earned only one half of the salary, but I was still richer than anybody else.

I decided to rent a house by the sea in Zorritos, a small village of fishermen half on hour away from the city.

I used to hold lessons only twice a week; I had plenty of time to read, rest and have a swim every now and then.

In Zorritos I met Ethel; she was a nineteen-year-old girl about to marry a fisherman fifteen years older than her. She used to work as a waitress in her mother's restaurant and look after her brothers and their house. Her father had left them.

One night, on the beach, I asked her: «Are you in love with the man you are going to marry?»

She must have thought that it was a silly question and stared at me, motionless. «What do you mean by "are you in love"?»

One week later she ran away from home and came to me.

«I don't love him and I don't want to marry him. If my mother finds out, she'll kill me. She has already arranged everything!»

I decided to step in, letting the dust settle. I talked to her mother: her daughter was young and had the right to lead a different life.

She looked at me surprised. «What life?»

Ethel wanted to go to University, so we used to go to the fishermen and sell them jelly to raise the money necessary for the courses. We would walk on the beach, talking about anything and making plans together. She started to read lots of books. Now she is working in a little restaurant and is renting rooms to the tourists. She has refurbished an abandoned space, a tiny wooden house with palm trees reaching out to the sea. She has seen many fishermen, but got married to none.

IV. Tumbes

After a couple of relaxing months spent in front of the sea, I decided to come back to the city. It was very hot in Tumbes, but at least there were meetings and events even after seven p.m. I had had enough of reading books and talking to fish. I wanted to rent a house and eventually found a huge one: eight rooms, three bathrooms, a garden, a terrace and a spacious kitchen. It was beautiful, but too big and expensive for me. The landlady offered me a small one and the rent was one hundred and fifty dollars. I immediately paid the deposit and assured her I would move there the following week. When I came back she told me she had already rented it. "What a pity," I thought. Then she offered me the big house at the same price. She hadn't rented it yet, so I immediately accepted and for a moment I felt like a matron.

My house was used as a school first, then as a hospital and even as the Ecuadorian consulate in Peru. It was amazing, perhaps a little too much: what would I do with all that space? A renovation would have been too expensive, and it was so big that you could hear the echo of the steps of the people passing by. I didn't know what to do and the only solution was to fill it up with people!

So I started to desperately search for new friends. I saw a street full of craftsmen: it was perfect for my purpose. I

bought some flowers and incenses. I made friends with the woman selling them. Her name was Carmen, she was from Trujillo, she was Buddhist and used to sleep in a hotel with her husband. She was perfect for me.
«Listen, Carmen, I have a huge house. You and your husband can both come and stay at my house.»
Carmen smiled brightly. Forty years old, five children: her dream was to save money aside.

There were already ten of us in the big house in Alfonso Ugarte road: Carmen, her husband, other craftsmen and some tourists passing by who were looking for accommodation. There was a lot of space. However, we needed beds, wardrobes, fans, chairs, sofas, dishes, cutlery and glasses. Such an investment made the owner of the furniture shop down the street very happy. That night my guests arrived together with their children, the most wonderful gift. We played games, ran in the garden and peacefully slept until sunrise.
Some days after, Santiago, Carmen's husband, told me that there were some young boys living on the streets. They were all bootblacks and slept in a single room with no light, no water and no toilet.
«That's horrible,» I said.
«A woman lets them in, but only at night. They bring some cardboard and use them as mattresses. When they need a shower, they just dive into the river.»

I didn't need to hear any more. I decided to welcome them in my house – we had plenty of room – I could not shut my eyes.
«Okay, Santiago,» I said «how many are they?»
«I'd have five or six of them first, just to see if it works. They must get used to the house routines. The rest is up to you.»
This was turning out to be interesting.
There was a new little boy every night. There was a strict discipline in the house, it looked like barracks: I used to fix doors and windows and took care of the rent and bills. Carmen supervised everything. Some of them swept the floors, others cooked and did the washing up. The boys cleaned up the house. In the evenings, we had endless parties in the garden with some music and beer. It became a sort of community centre with a guaranteed accommodation. John dealt with the newly arrived, Santiago selected them and Carmen provided them with a broom. Everything was just so beautiful words cannot explain.
I had a big room for myself on the first floor, overlooking the garden. My door was always open and, when I was away, my bed could be used by the person who first conquered it. I can't remember the number of people actually living in the house. We had established an atypical matriarchy, with twenty or thirty little boys staying with us.

Besides me, there was Carmen, Jenny – a lawyer – and Carla, a girl who was studying to become a nurse.
The house management had its rules: all the boys woke up at six in the morning, had a shower and went to work. At around eleven, some of them came back home with some money so that Carmen could go to the market and buy something to eat. Somebody helped her. There used to be huge lunch and dinner tables. There was music, TV, new people coming over, people sharing experiences or telling stories.
We used to go to the beach on Saturdays and Sundays. We were such an original group. We supported each other and fought together against the far-reaching racism. There were lots of youngsters struggling to make ends meet when I worked at the University, which, by the way, was a miracle in such a tremendously racist and classist society. I often thought of many friends of mine working in NGOs who earned high salaries and lived locked down in their houses. We had no bars and you only needed to open the front door to discover our world.

V. The prisons

It was afternoon, the postman handed me a letter: I was invited by the government to join a workgroup within the National Truth and Reconciliation Commission. It was a project developed by President Valentín Paniagua to allow the citizens to report on the abuses committed by the State and/or guerrilla groups. They were looking for an expert in Political Science working in the academic world. I was what they were looking for.

In 2001, the former dictator Alberto Fujimori resigned via fax while he was escaping eastwards and eventually found shelter in Japan. Alessandro Toledo became the president of a country restoring democracy after a twenty-year civil war (1980-2000), countless coups and a difficult financial situation. The country hoped for a change in the regime embodied by a man dressed up as an Incan and openly claiming his cross-bred, popular origins.

Alessandro Toledo carried out a famous protest march, called *De los cuatro suyos*, which contributed to the fall of the dictatorship of Vladimir Montesino-Alberto Fujimori. People trusted him because he talked and dressed like them.

Under his government, then, the Truth Commission had to cope with two decades of violence. Nobody knew why.

Some peculiar debates were held. Victims of violent acts and persecutors sat side by side. People defending criminals and victims of torture, all officially aiming at 'reconciling spirits'. The tension was so high that you could inhale it. The President of the Court didn't know which Saint to pray to.

«Do you see that man?» a woman once asked me. «He took my child away.»

One week later, we were all morally torn apart. The tortures perpetrated by Senderists[5], Comuneros[6]and armed forces were accurately described. At that time I was asked by the Commission lawyers to collect the testimonies of five (alleged) terrorists locked up in jail.

Accompanied by a lawyer, I met the partner of a convict who had been in prison for ten years and whose judgement was still pending.

«Ten years without any trial? That's unbelievable!»

An informer accused him of being a member of the Sendero command. The policemen, hooded up, entered his home, arrested and tortured him. Some years after, the informer retraced his steps claiming that the man was innocent and that he had made up some random names

---

[5] Followers of Sendero Luminoso (officially known as 'Communist Party of Peru on the shining path of Mariátegui'), a Peruvian Maoist-inspired war organisation.

[6] The way in which Charles V used to call the people of some Spanish rebel villages in the 16th century and the people from the Paraguayan and New Granada (Colombia) villages which rose up against Spain in the 18th century.

under torture. The informer was set free, but the young man still stayed in prison.
«He was not even 18 years old,» his wife told us.
«They entered our home and smashed everything. They even closed me in a room and tried to rape me. Then they put a hood on José and took him away. I cried for days, but there was nothing I could do. On top of that, people looked at us in fear, their gazes implied that, after all, we deserved it. It was a civil war and the motto was 'punish one, teach a hundred'. Who could this apply to?"
The lawyer and I headed to the prison, in silence.
«This is your case,» he said. "You're Italian: write whatever you want.»

I found myself in a room with José. He was just thirty years old, ten of which spent in jail. After having listened to his story, I asked: «José, what do you want me to do? Shall we start the compensation procedure or would you like to ask for a pardon?»
«I just want to get out of here.»
When I left, I hugged him. «I'll do everything I can, José.»
I wrote the word INNOCENT on the dossier and handed it to the head of the Commission. Justice sometimes reaches, eventually, even the godforsaken places on the Earth. If setting an innocent free after ten years in prison can be regarded as justice.

VI. Giulia

A few days later, I was walking across the city when someone called me: it was José, he was set free! It was amazing! I hugged him and invited him to my home for a chat. «What will you do now?» I asked him.

«I'll buy a taxi to help sustain my family, but now I'll tell you another story.»

«Tell me José, I'm all ears.»

«When I was arrested, I was brought to a room with twenty other boys. We were all blindfolded with our hands tied. The policemen came in, kicked us in the face, in the stomach, dragged us by the hair and tortured us. The most awful thing were the cries of other boys, because I thought: "*Now it's my turn to die!*" In those moments you don't belong to anyone, you know? If you faint, they throw water at your face, because they take delight in your fear. They are sadistic. Then they told us that we were going somewhere else, and we were happy. I can't tell you why: it was something irrational, but I hoped that the tortures would end at least during the journey. It was like having a change of scenery, finding a new hope. They packed us in their vans, we were full of bruises, blood flew out of our bodies and they did not stop insulting us. As soon as we left the city, one of the vans stopped, followed by the others. We could hear the noise of the engines and the

echo of their laughter. We sat in silence, preparing ourselves for the worst. In the distance, the sea waves were crashing on the rocks.
Giulia was sitting next to me, trying to hug me, but she couldn't. She leant her head against my chest, our panting breaths followed each other. They opened the van door with crazy laughter. "Come on, beautiful guerrilla girl, let us see your revolution!"
We immediately understood that they were referring to her. Giulia screamed, but we couldn't do anything: they hit us with the gun barrels, as if it were a slaughterhouse. We thought that torture was the worst thing, while actually the worst was yet to come. We could hear her screams and we writhed in pain. Her screams were piercing blades, then silence fell. Those pigs kept on laughing and abusing her. Come on, Giulia, cry out loud! Let your anger out, don't restrain it! Laughter and rapes, rapes and laughter. Eventually, I escaped and jumped out of the van. "You, bastards, murderers, mother ... " A gun barrel hit me at the temples, "Giulia, where are you?" I thought of her smile and fainted in the water.
I woke up some hours later, locked up in a cell. I cried for days, «Giulia, what did they do to you?»
«José,» I told him, «I can't believe it's true.»
«It's true. You must believe in me.»
«Did Giulia denounce this violence?» I asked.

«Of course, all the newspapers published the news. And the policemen were all rewarded for their honour. What could a girl charged with terrorism expect from the State? Justice?
Eventually, she was set free, because she was innocent. “Sorry, we were wrong, we cancel the sentence and you, little girl, go back home. Your dolls are waiting for you.”
Giulia was sixteen years old when she was caught, and when she was released her mother could hardly recognise her. Now she lives here in Tumbes, outside the city. If you want to meet her, I'll give you her address. I'm sure she will be glad to see you.»
«Thank you, José, I'll see her.»
I was shocked. A girl raped by a herd of criminals. I talked about this event to the people passing by, and everyone remembered it. So why did nobody talk about it?
Some days later I called Giulia to ask her if she wanted to meet me.
«They were seventeen pigs and raped me cruelly. I was bleeding everywhere and fainted several times, but they threw water at my face, because they wanted me to see their faces. They dismembered me alive. I had nightmares for many years. Their threats, their looks, their laughter. I remember my father's face when I left the prison: he had absorbed my pain. He kept his head down and could hardly speak.
“What have they done to you?” he asked me.

And then the people didn't greet me anymore. In the city I often met those pigs. They attended the Mass with their wives and children and looked at me as if to say: "You asked for it, baby. I bet you liked it." That's why I came here outside the city. Here I can isolate myself, nobody knows me. I was just a young girl, I was sixteen years old. They were never imprisoned for their crime. I would like to kill them all. In this case, I wouldn't mind being imprisoned once again.»

«Then call me, Giulia, I'll come with you.»

VII. Journey to Quito

At the end of November 2002, a Latin-American meeting of indigenous groups against the ALCA (Free Trade Area of the Americas) was held in Quito. I knew little or nothing at all about this topic and, especially, about the organisation of the local communities.

Then I moved to the beautiful capital of Ecuador, located at about 2,800 meters above sea level, to see what was happening there. I took a bus along the border with Peru and travelled through cities full of coconut and banana trees, which reminded me of Africa.

Once in Quito, I was welcomed by many natives who had walked for weeks to say NO to the ALCA, TLC (Free Trade Agreement) and the American imperialism. For the first time, I noticed such a radical commitment along the streets. It was the first time that I saw women wearing skirts called 'polleras', bearing their children tied on their shoulders like rebel bundles.

Proud looks, fists up. Nothing could stop them.

Ecuador hoped for a revolution with Lucho Gutiérrez, who stood as a candidate for the Presidency and had promised to support the indigenous groups, in addition to social reforms and the opposition to the free trade agreement, which actually promoted a new economic colonisation

disguised as fake progress. The TLC suffocated the countries through its neo-liberal initiatives. First, it encouraged monoculture: sugar cane, coffee, bananas or cocoa. Then it lowered or raised the interest rates to increase or decrease the export volumes. The lower classes lived at the mercy of temporary employment agreements, while the ruling classes became richer and richer.
Bolivia and Paraguay, for example, were as rich as Switzerland or Germany, but their ruling classes had sold cheaply their natural resources and opposed a fair distribution of wealth. Thus the natives walked to Quito - the capital of one of the smallest and most fascinating countries in the world - to defend a life worth being led.
The other presidential candidate was Álvaro Noboa from Guayaquil, a landowner, banana exporter and one of the richest men in the world, involved in mafia associations. He promoted economic agreements with the United States, as well as the introduction of a neo-liberal model in the Country. High-quality education for few people. Being the owner of many television channels, he was very popular among the people, passing off his populism as a form of participatory democracy.
The electoral campaign was very violent and the police ended up assaulting the native women.
The tear gas intoxicated the children who vomited everywhere along the street, and there was a general harry.

In that period I met Ana, a nice architect from Paris. We got lost in Quito as we talked about Guayasamín[7] and Manuelita Sáenz[8].

Eventually, Lucho Gutiérrez won the elections. For the first time in the history of the Ecuadorian republic, indigenous men and women were elected ministers and became members of the parliament. Ana and I celebrated this event together in the squares of the capital. It was hard to defeat Noboa, but we managed to do it!

---

[7]Oswaldo Guayasamín (Quito, 6 July1919 – Baltimora, 10 March1999) was an Ecuadorian painter.

[8]Manuela Sáenz de Thorne, also known as the 'Libertadora del Libertador' (Quito, 27 December 1797 – Paita, Peru, 23 November 1856), was the lover of Simón Bolívar, the South American revolutionary commander.

VIII. New Year's Day at the seaside

The end of the year was approaching and I wanted to get to know other areas of Peru; I had a contract at national scale, therefore I could request a transfer.

One day the Head of the courses called from the embassy and told me: «There is a vacant position at the University of Cuzco, would you like to have a change of scenery?»

It was more than a simple change of scenery! I would live at 3,399 meters above sea level, surrounded by the Andes, a few hundred kilometres away from Titicaca, the highest and most fascinating lake in the world. I would see Tipón, Sacsayhuaman, Ollantaytambo and the legendary Machu Picchu! I would coordinate the courses at the Saint Anthony University; since a colleague was about to go back to Italy and his position was left vacant.

Before moving to Cuzco, I wanted to spend some a few days at the seaside, in Máncora. It was the first time that I celebrated New Year's Day at the beach, it was late December and people were sunbathing on the beach. At midnight we dived into the sea and then, full of energy, I travelled to the legendary city of Cuzco.

IX. Travel to Cuzco

While at the University of Tumbes relaxation was the name of the game, in Cuzco everybody worked hard.
The Head of the Italian courses was called 'the slave driver', and it was easy to understand why. I looked for her in her office and she welcomed me kindly; she told me that in the language department of the university there were about four thousand students who were studying French, English, Quechua and Italian, and she had great expectations of me. I was pleased, but I thought that my task dealt with educational aspects, but she explained: «You must check the work of your colleagues.»
«I don’t understand.»
«Well, you just have to visit the classrooms, see how the professors work and then send me a report.»
I shuddered; so much for the ‘slave driver'!
She introduced me to Carolina, a Peruvian colleague who had been teaching there for years. I offered her a coffee and asked: «The head of the courses has told me that I have to check you. But what is her purpose?»
Carolina and I held lessons with such enthusiasm that the students increasingly grew in number, however this was not enough for the slave driver: she wanted us to make up for the strikes and holidays. At Easter she wanted to reduce our salary because we had a one-week holiday.

This sent me into a rage and I cornered the head of the courses: if she had not granted us the holidays due, we would have vacationed anyway. She eventually accepted our request, so I could travel to Bolivia, one of the poorest and most fascinating countries in the world.

X. Almond eyes

After having been in Bolivia, I travelled to Chile, Argentina, Uruguay, Paraguay, Colombia, Venezuela and Brazil. As soon as I had some spare time, I used to take a plane or catch a bus and explore the southern part of the world. The Andes, Patagonia, Caribe, Chaco.

One day, before going to Chile, I met a girl in Cuzco who seemed familiar to me. She was Maca'n and she loved poetry, art and painting: it was love at first sight. «I'm going to Chile. Would you like to come with me?» I asked her.

Maca'n accepted immediately: she hastily packed her bags and we moved together southwards. Arequipa, Tacna, Iquique, Valdivia; we had a long journey by bus looking at the landscape and smiling at life.

Santiago greeted us warmly and we visited La Moneda, Allende's house and the Neruda museums. We got in touch with some members of the MIR, the Revolutionary Left Movement, and were fascinated by those people who had not given up their fight since the time of Pinochet. In Valparaíso, a group of activists welcomed us into their house and wanted us to remain there. We spent the nights drinking, smoking and eating tasty sandwiches with ham and salmon. And then we journeyed to the funicular railway, Miguel Hernández and the walks through the city.

We were told that in Valdivia, south of the town, there were some frescoes by Orozco[9], so we visited the city hit by the tsunami.

We saw the point reached by the waves and shuddered. The water had retreated and people had died, because they did not know that the waves were returning with an incredible violence. A dreadful scream and thousands of lives taken away in an instant.

Maca'n asked me: «Why did they hit so violently?» And this reminded her of the *desaparecidos* of the Esma, their mothers protesting along the streets as well as of the songs of Victor Jara sung at the stadium.

Then we reached Chiloé, Port Mont and there we took a ferry to Castro. We landed on a beautiful Patagonian island with pile dwellings in the middle of the sea.

People used their canoes as means of transport and went up simple wooden ladders to enter their houses. We thought of our heavily guarded houses and felt a great sadness.

Eventually, we arrived in Ancud, where we spent some days on the beach together with the fishermen. They ate the *loco*[10] and finally I dived into the water.

---

[9] *José Clemente Orozco* (Ciudad Guzmán, 23 November 1883 - Mexico City, 7 September 1949), was a Mexican painter specialising in wall painting, to the extent they started the so-called *Mexican Mural Renaissance*. Orozco was the most sophisticated Mexican muralist and used to represent the human pain.

[10] It is a kind of mollusc similar to limpets.

I felt the cold in my bones like a steel blade, but I was happy to look at the world from that perspective. Maca’n approached some clumsy penguins: they were beautiful, small and plump.

Then we travelled towards the lake region, the border between Chile and Argentina, with its swamps, waterfalls and nature reserves. I hoped that a Mapuche offered us a tea in his tent. Macan's eyes smiled at the world and further enhanced the beauty of the surrounding nature.

XI. Buenos Aires

Once back in Chile, Maca'n and I decided to rent a little house together in Lima, precisely in Breña, a wonderful, residential district.

As soon as we had some spare days, we used to ask each other: «Colombia, Brazil or Venezuela?»

We celebrated the 2004 New Year's Day in Buenos Aires.

I wanted to travel by bus but Maca'n was shocked: «By bus? It'll take us four days!»

She looked at me and smiled, and always pandered to me as often as she could. Four days of travel by bus, that was something crazy!

At the end of the journey, we were worn out due to the fatigue and the high temperature.

At the border with Chile, a boy told me: «I have some smuggled CDs, I earn a living with them. They will take them away from me, but not from you! Would you mind putting them in your luggage?»

I told the policeman that those CDs were my favourite music, but I did not look like a fanatic supporter of the most disparate music in the world.

«And where do you live? In a disco?»

At the border with Argentina, an officer halted a boy who was travelling with us: he had no money, so we immediately collected five hundred dollars. His visa was eventually accepted, hurrah!

In Buenos Aires, we were greeted by Fabiana at her big house. She had studied in Milan and knew some friends of ours.

«You can stay here as long as you wish," she told us, and we took her at her words.

We stayed at hers for about one month; every Thursday we gathered in the square with the protesting mothers. They did not want any compensation, they just wanted their children's bodies back. Then we visited the ESMA, the aviation military school where the '*milicos*' [11] had imprisoned and tortured thousands of innocent young people.

This gave us goosebumps: we listened to the news on the radio, shared the social protests and watched *Garage Olimpo* at the cinema. Everything was emotionally strong and violent; the history of Argentina is tragic.

At night we used to go to San Telmo and La Boca, dancing the tango and singing the celebration of life of Mercedes Sosa.

One day I asked Maca'n: «Would you like to travel southwards?», so we headed to Mar del Plata, where we met Yanick, a Peruvian friend of ours who was waiting for

---

[11] Soldiers. Cops in a pejorative sense.

us. She gave us the keys to an apartment and we spent a wonderful week at the seaside.
Then we continued our journey southwards towards Porto Tombo in the penguin nature reserve, our dear friends!
During our full immersion into the local nature, we could not miss the Patagonian glaciers of Perito Moreno. We drove there by bus and met French, Germans, Ukrainians and Chileans, an incredible mix of languages and culture; we got along so well together that it looked like an organised tour.
Eventually, we reached Perito Moreno at night with an impressive full moon and suddenly we heard some cracks. They sounded like gunshots, but actually it was the ice which got in contact with the sea. Then we met other guys in Ushuaia, the southernmost city in the world, in Tierra del Fuego.
We looked like penniless hippies, while some people were landing from a cruise ship: it was a striking contrast!
Gennaro, a boy from Naples who was studying in Mexico City, was the entertainer of the group. Maca'n had brought along some of her paintings, and set up an improvised exhibition along the street. It was a good start for an artist, in the land of all the fires. We were also impressed by the prison where the political opponents were kept.
After some relaxation in Patagonia, Maca'n and I decided to return to Buenos Aires. But there was no place for us on the buses, and the flights were too expensive.

«What about hitchhiking?»
«Have you gone mad? It is a journey of three thousand kilometres!»
She initially disagreed, but was eventually ready for this adventure.
On the highway we did not have to wait too long: the truckers gave us a lift. They used their walkie-talkies to call their colleagues: «We are transporting two girls who are going to Buenos Aires, can you give them a lift?»
We got on and off those twelve-wheeled monsters which carried milk, fruit, wine and electric appliances. They were provided with all the comforts: music, beds and food.

Fabiana was not there to welcome us in Buenos Aires, therefore we went to San Telmo to look for a hotel, when I suddenly heard someone calling me. I could not believe it! It was Francesca, one dear friend of mine!
«What are you doing here?» I asked her.
«I'm working for an NGO which promotes social development, and what about you, girls? Where are you going with those heavy backpacks? There is space enough in my house, would you like to come?»
It was a blessing! After several weeks spent on buses, we could not believe that we were going to have a true bedroom! Francesca was preparing the dinner singing: «*Bellooo, bello e impossibileeeeeeee! La la la la la... e il*

tuo sapor medio orientaleeeeeee! Belloooooo e irraggiungibileeeeee...[12]»

[12] A song by Gianna Nannini, an Italian singer.

XII. Montevideo and the environs

After Buenos Aires, we decided to visit Uruguay, the homeland of Eduardo Galeano and Mario Benedetti. In Montevideo, we were welcomed by 'negrita', one friend of ours, who kindly hosted us at her wonderful house.

The country, after decades of dictatorship and conservative governments, was going to experience one of the most glorious moments of its revolutionary history. José Mujica, leader of Tupamaros, a guerrilla group which fought against the military dictatorship and the 1973 coup, was about to be appointed President of the Senate and of the Republic.

Montevideo was full of red flags and everybody – on the buses, in the cafes, along the street – was happy. A man tortured by the soldiers had been elected President of the Republic. Now he was the head of the army, namely of his torturers.

Maca'n and I celebrated this event along the streets of Montevideo, waving red flags, and had a toast in front of the house of Garibaldi.

Our friend worked in a theatre and allowed us to attend all the shows. We were happy and wanted those moments to last forever.

After our stay in Uruguay, we could not miss Paraguay, so deeply affected by Stroessner's military dictatorship [13] which lasted forty years and resulted in a severe economic crisis. Previously, Paraguay had a flowering economy: the first railway line in Latin America, the first autonomous enterprises, plenty of natural resources. And then the 'War of the Triple Alliance' against Argentina, Uruguay and Brazil broke out.

History repeats itself everywhere: the European countries encourage populism and then earn a lot of money from the sale of weapons, food and ammunition. And when the country has been brought to its knees, they take advantage of the reconstruction works.

Bolivia, Paraguay, Afghanistan: the poor are getting poorer, while the rich are getting richer.

In Assunción we met some young supporters of Guevarism who were putting their lives at risk to oppose the regime.

One day we were told: «Here in Paraguay there are the Iguazu Falls, the most beautiful and the largest waterfalls in the world, you should see them!»

Maca'n and I smiled. «We cannot miss them!»

Eventually, we travelled from Paraguay to Parana, in Brazil.

---

[13] Alfredo Stroessner Matiauda (3 November 1912, Encarnación, Paraguay - 16 August 2006, Brasilia, Brazil) was a Paraguayan politician and soldier, president and dictator of his country from 15 August 1954 to 3 February 1989.

Across the border, we experienced the highest forms of smuggling on the bridge 'de la amistad' which joined Paraguay with Argentina and Brazil. Everybody was running wildly, lifting and taking the parcels down the ropes, then the crazy rides on taxi: cigarettes, bicycles, blenders, microwaves, televisions, radios, mobile phones, bras and blackberries. Anything and everything.

Maca'n and I looked for the cheapest hotel and eventually chose one full of transgender people.

The surrounding environment was moving and the waterfalls were impressive. It took us a number of days to recover and start our journey homeward.

XIII. Chaco

After those impressive waterfalls, we returned to Assunción and then looked for a bus to Santa Cruz, Bolivia.

«It'll take about eighteen hours,» we were told, «You will have to cross the whole Chaco»

«Will we stop somewhere for dinner?»

They looked at us perplexed. «For dinner? In the desert, there are only snakes, jaguars and stray dogs.»

«Oh, thank you.»

We had a look at the bus and did not know whether to laugh or cry. It looked like an old crock with four wheels patched together. Oh my God, eighteen hours by bus!

The luggage rack was full. One half of the travellers were foreigners, while the others were local inhabitants, including women with '*polleras*' and taciturn men.

«A journey of eighteen hours? Well, let's start the countdown!»

After the first five hours, I asked the driver if we could stop for a coffee and he looked at me stunned. «The journey will be long, girl».

«But the toilet is out of order and the smell is unbearable.»

«It's dangerous out there, there are snakes and jaguars.»

Later on, we were at the end of our tether, we just wanted to stop, stretch our legs and smoke a cigarette. Suddenly we heard a ticking on the glass: tick-tack-tick-tack. It was the rain, tick-tack-tick-tack. It was really hot and rain was welcomed like a blessing, tick-tack-tick-tack. At first, the rain was gentle tick-tack-tick-tack, then it sounded like a machine gun, tick-tack-tick-tack. We all fell silent, tick-tack-tick-tack, the rain became heavier and heavier, tick-tack-tick-tack, it turned into a river, tick-tack-tick-tack, then into a lake, tick-tack-tick-tack and eventually into a sea tick-tack-tick-tack.

The bus moved through the water, tick-tack-tick-tack, it did not stop raining, tick-tack-tick-tack we looked out of the windows and the water was everywhere, tick-tack-tick-tack, a deep silence, tick-tack-tick-tack and the bus staggered, tick-tack-tick-tack. Our journey had started twenty hours earlier but we had covered less than one-third of the total distance, tick-tack-tick-tack we were stuck in the middle of the desert, tick-tack-tick-tack the water covered the wheels, tick-tack-tick-tack, we got out of the bus in the middle of the swamp and the driver took out the shovels.

«Someone help me shovel and you find some branches to light a fire!» «Where is the bridge?» a Swedish girl asked me.

Maca'n tried to reassure the travellers, I helped shovel the mud away and then looked for some wood. I did anything to stay calm.

Eventually, we recovered our journey and stopped after five or six kilometres. Tick-tack-tick-tack the river in flood, tick-tack-tick-tack «Where is the bridge?», tick-tack-tick-tack no one answered.
Then we reached a wrecked bridge and the driver told us: «Get out of the bus. I'll try to take the bus to the other side of the river.»
While it was crossing the river, the soil crumbled and the bus was hanging in the air, then we pushed it like a raft. The Bolivian women were staring at us: we were smoking, shovelling the mud away, joking with boys and pushing the buses. What kind of women were we?
The initial eighteen hours of travel became fifty, and finally one hundred. One afternoon the bus laid stuck in the mud bent at almost ninety degrees, tick-tack-tick-tack, we got out of the bus through the windows and Maca'n was sleeping and remained on the bus. The driver tried to continue the journey: he turned the engine on and the bus started to move.
«Macaaaa'n!», we cried and then we saw a pair of almond eyes out the window! We took a step forward and slid into the mud up to the groin. It reminded me of the Tarzan movie that I watched when I was a child.
Too many bridges had collapsed and the driver sent an SOS; two mechanical shovels arrived, were attached to the bus and put it in motion once again. We walked out like zombies.

We slowly reached the border with Bolivia.
The official was not there due to the flood, and the borderline had turned into a river in full spate. Only few of us could swim and I offered to carry the luggage and food across the border.
The bus emptied, the driver took a run-up from Paraguay and drove into the river at full speed. I feared that it might crashed, the wheels reached Bolivia and ... BRUMMM! The driver pressed down on the accelerator in the water. I do not know how it was possible but, in spite of the debris and mud, the driver took the bus to the other side of the street.

After the tragic experience in the Chaco region, we looked for a hot shower that would have brought a smile even on the face of the saddest man in the world!

XIV. Santa Cruz

We crossed the border without any stamp on our passports, and the driver said: «You must go to the police station in Santa Cruz to notify your entry to Bolivia within forty-eight hours.»

And we took his advice.

«Good evening, we are seven foreigners and we crossed the border with Paraguay. There was no officer there, so we don't have any entry visa.»

Evidently, they regarded us as easy targets and had a great idea.

«Now we'll take your passports and will return them to you against a penalty payment of one hundred and fifty dollars for the illegal crossing of the border.»

«That was a swamp, not a border!»

One hundred and fifty dollars multiplied by seven was a considerable sum.

"You, corrupted cops, give us our passports back!» Maca'n began to cry.

Obviously, it was not a great idea to threaten policemen in a police station, so they raised the bar. «Now we'll bang you up!»

It was a tough fight and someone was already taking out their credit card. But suddenly I had an idea.

«Now we'll call the press and denounce you!»

Maca'n realised that they were in trouble and piled it on:
«Torturers! Murderers!»
She was so brave and courageous, but five policemen dragged her outside the police station.
«Don't do her any harm or I'll kill you!»
They did not know what to do and were more frightened than us, so we went away and decided to return the following day.
We came back accompanied by a lawyer and duly informed. They did not request one hundred and fifty dollars any more, however they still asked for a nominal remuneration, since they were doing us a favour. I told them that we just wanted our passports back, and they started to sweat with cold from fear.
«That's OK just this once!»
Maca'n jumped for joy, Chaco docet, hurrah!

XV. La Paz

We rejoiced and then parted ways with a big hug.
Someone was heading to La Paz, others towards the south of Bolivia; those five days in the desert, the misadventure at the police station and the walks across Santa Cruz were unforgettable.
We took the bus to La Paz and were involved in a social protest.
In Cochabamba the buses were stuck, stones and tyres were burning in the middle of the street. Maca'n was tired and wanted to go home.
«I don't want to spend night after night outdoors!»
We got out of the bus and walked many miles. Some abusive cars pierced the roadblocks, but they were too expensive and dangerous.
The Bolivians were going through a radical social change and occupied railways, airports and highways. There were clashes with the police and even corpses along the streets.
We met fanatical people and feared that they could kill us.
«Let's take a taxi and reach the checkpoints, I don't want to stay here!» Maca'n suggested.
We were really frightened; we talked to a man. «I know a rarely trodden street,» he told us. «If you are willing to take the risk, I'll help you.»

We drove hastily across a dusty path, a series of rises and falls in the Andes, and were afraid of dying. Suddenly we reached a checkpoint, some boys were standing there, holding stones and sticks. Pum! The first glass breaks. Pum! The second breaks too!

«Close your eyes and cover your faces, girls!»

Pum! The van is full of splinters. Fortunately, we did not run over anyone, because we were madly escaping at full speed while the boys were trying to stop us. We supported their fight, but we also wanted to get away from that chaos. Eventually, we arrived in La Paz late at night and entered the first hotel that we saw.

The streets looked like a battlefield: tear gas, barricades, gun shots. I suggested we stay there for a few days, but Maca'n looked at me bewildered.

«I'll go home tomorrow!»

The following day we looked for another taxi willing to pass through the checkpoints.

That was another great adventure; the driver took secondary streets, but we always bumped into some boys who threw stones, and we felt like we were locked in a cage.

We heartily supported the struggle of the Bolivians but, after a journey of three months across South America, we wanted to go home. I missed my friends and Maca'n missed her house by the sea.

We drove along Lake Titicaca and through the Andes. After the last checkpoint, we saw Peru.

«Drive faster! We will be home soon!»

And Maca'n shouted: «Home, sweet home!»

XVI. La Cantuta

In Lima we lived in the Breña district, and the drivers were frightened when I asked them to take me home at night. «Be careful, miss, it's dangerous there.»

In our street there were Juan, the pharmacist, and Maradona, who sold tobacco and groceries. On the corner there was a large market where on Sundays we ate *ceviche* and drank *chicha morada*; it was a simple and beautiful life.

I held lectures at La Cantuta University, which joined the struggle against the dictatorship of Alberto Fujimori, and where the death squads had kidnapped and tortured nine students and one professor. With this action, the State addressed the whole movement: punish one, teach a hundred, however the students, on the contrary, brought the struggle to a higher level. When I went to the faculty, I saw students holding microphones that occupied canteens and offices, reciting mottos against the mafia.

One day, during a protest against the TLC, many students were wildly beaten and arrested. I was called and rushed to the police station; they had bruises everywhere, I called a lawyer and assisted them in the trial. When they were released, they were welcomed as heroes into the classrooms: it was the proper reward for having defended the right to study.

XVII. Caracas

In February 2005 there was a social forum in Caracas that I did not want to miss; people came from all over the world to a city which was a synonym for rebellion. The right wing, supported by the CIA, tried several times to suffocate a social revolution, reducing the gas supply to the houses. But people came out in resistance, and the elderly started to burn chairs and cupboards to avoid the political ascent of the oligarchy.

Venezuela, with its impressive oil deposits, is one of the richest and most powerful countries in the world, however the wealth distribution is unfair and excludes most of the population. Only the members of a self-righteous class were entitled to education, healthcare and rights.

Then Hugo Chávez[14] said: «No more hypocrisy, no more privileges, no more social misery»; he promoted education, created shelters and soup kitchens, and called twenty thousand doctors from Cuba in exchange for oil. He offered scholarships to the Bolivian and Peruvian students. Therefore, it is not surprising that the right wing tried to hinder him.

---

[14]Hugo Rafael Chávez Frías (Sabaneta, 28 July 1954 - Caracas, 5 March 2013) was a Venezuelan politician and soldier. He was president of Venezuela from 1999 until his death, except for a brief coup in 2002.

Then the social forum took place in Caracas during the revolution. Hundreds of thousands of supporters from all over the world experienced fifteen days of revolutionary ecstasy.

I took a bus from Lima, arrived in Quito and then took a plane to Caracas. Everything was free there: trains, buses, canteens and the people's hugs along the streets. Then there were debates, dinners, parties, meetings and emotions. Twenty thousand Colombians were tired of the government of Uribe[15] as well as of a civil war which had lasted for forty years.

I attended a conference on Camillo Torres[16] and was fascinated by Lucho, a guerrilla from Bogota. He had fought for seventeen years in Colombia and Nicaragua, but eventually decided to continue the fight with other weapons.

«I'll wait for you in Bogota,» he said. «I would like to show you something.»

In Caracas I met some women of the Manuelita Sáenz feminist group, and they asked me to hold a lecture on the Italian and European feminist movement. It was really

---

[15]Álvaro Uribe Vélez (Medellín, 4 July 1952) is a Colombian politician and lawyer, President of Colombia from 2002 to 2010.

[16]Camilo Torres Restrepo (Bogotà, 3 February 1929 - Department of Santander, 15 February 1966) was a Colombian presbyter, guerrilla and revolutionary, founder of the Liberation Theology, co-founder of the first Faculty of Sociology and member of the Colombian National Liberation Army.

exciting, they were supported by some politicians, Carla Lonzi[17] docet.

«As soon as the revolution began, I left my husband,» one of them told me. «I still loved him, but I realised that I wanted more. I did not work or study, I did nothing except for the housework. So I left him and started to attend a sociology course, then I looked for a job and joined a feminist group. I owe all this to Chavez, I would give my life for him.»

Manuelita Saenz was the lover of Simón Bolívar[18]. During the struggle for independence against Spain in the 19th century, she left her husband to follow the man that she loved, and adhered to his revolutionary ideas. She took part in the battle of Ayacucho and fought on Sucre's side in Colombia, Bolivia and Quito. She used to ride a horse and hold a shotgun; she often saved the Libertador's life. Manuelita is the symbol of the revolt of women in the world. She always remained loyal to her ideas and died in exile in Paita, north of Peru. We felt her presence and her revolutionary strength, always by our side.

---

17 Carla Lonzi (Florence, 6 March 1931 - Milan, 2 August 1982) was an Italian writer, critic of art and feminist, who theorised self-awareness and sexual difference. She founded the Rivolta Femminile collective in the early Seventies.

18 Simón Bolívar (Caracas 1783 - San Pedro Alexandrino, Santa Marta, 1830) was a Venezuelan soldier and political leader. With José de San Martín he was the main promoter of the independence of Latin America. In the first decades of the 19th century in Latin America the Spanish and Portuguese colonies started to struggle for their independence from the homeland. Simón Bolívar, then a young Venezuelan patriot, led the liberation movement.

XVIII. Maracaibo and Santa Marta

After Caracas I decided to go to the seaside, so I eventually arrived in Maracaibo, the hottest city in the world. Cockroaches came out from the sewer covers on the streets, then climbed on sidewalks and walls.

There I met a French friend of mine, Paul, who helped me look for a hotel. We found few neat accommodation; the owner welcomed us with enthusiasm.

«We have killed them all!» and I saw a multitude of dead cockroaches! There were thousands of them and I almost fainted. My friend took the broom and swept them out of sight, we heard "crack, crack" and the owner said: «Come on girl, are you afraid of dead animals?»

Well, I was, and I was writhing in disgust.

Paul and I spent nights talking to each other and walking along the streets of Maracaibo, then I decided to continue my journey to the north of Colombia. At the station of the buses to Santa Marta, I met Pablo, a boy from Argentina, who wanted to sunbathe and relax. We decided to look for accommodation, and finally rented a beautiful house.

Pablo was reading *Open veins* ... by Eduardo Galeano, a book which deeply influenced my life. He told me that the *milicos* had taken his parents away when he was just five years old and had never seen them again. *Desaparecidos*, like another thirty thousand people in Argentina under the dictatorship of Videla[19].

One night we were on the beach and he pointed at Cuba.

«If I could swim to Cuba,» he said, «I would like to go there to search for the souls of my parents!»

---

[19] Jorge Rafael Videla Redondo (Mercedes, 2 August 1925 - Buenos Aires, 17 May 2013) was an Argentine general and politician, dictator and, de facto, 42nd president of Argentina between 1976 and 1981, during the military regime called National Reorganization Process; he was responsible for crimes against humanity, especially for the murder of the *desaparecidos*. He came to power with a coup which deposed Isabelita Perón. His government was characterised by the violation of human rights and fights along the border with Chile which were going to escalate into a war.

XIX. Bogotà

After Santa Marta I travelled to Carthage and Medellín and eventually arrived in Bogota, where I called Lucho.
«Hi, I am a friend of Camillo. Do you remember me?»
He hosted me in his house for a couple of weeks; we used to go to the cinema, the theatre and walk along the city. He talked to me about Raúl Gómez Jattin and read me his poems: «I promise not to love you eternally ...»
Lucho was a guerrilla and a great poet as well. He told me that one of his comrades was killed by a policeman on 8th March while she was occupying the canteen of a factory.
«She fell right in front of me, but we had to flee, we were surrounded by the policemen who were shooting at us.»
He told me her story and hugged me. «She was a fierce feminist, the look in your eyes reminds me of her, I'll never forget her.»
I visited Bogota with its colours, the charming Candelaria, the scents of late summer, the house of Manuelita.
I walked southwards to Pereira, with its coffee plantations, then Cali, Popayán and the border with Ecuador.

Anna, the "French" architect, was waiting for me in Quito. She still devoted herself to poetry and the support of transgender communities.

I took a bus back to Tumbes and slept at Ethel's house. I hugged once again that girl, who had built her own dreams and desires among the palms on the shoreline. I closed my eyes and focused on the look of the girl who had escaped from home. A lesson for all those who are locked up in virtual cages. Still anchored to Carla Lonzi, sometimes we are not able to open the windows and throw ourselves into the world.

XX. Castro Castro

Once back in Lima, I resumed my work as an Italian professor at the University and the Institute of Culture.
One day, Carmen Rosa, a colleague of mine, told me: «Did you know that we have signed an agreement with the prison and we may hold lectures there as well?»
It was a great opportunity: teaching to common and political prisoners, helping them get an education qualification that could reduce their penalty. Seven to one, seven years of study and one of freedom.

In order to be authorised to hold lectures in prison, you had to meet some bureaucratic requirements: the licence from the Institute and the Embassy as well as an invitation from the prison and the NGO. Finally, we were admitted.
Carlos Alvarez, head of the NGO, met me at the Institute of Culture and took me to the famous Castro Castro, the high-security prison in Lima. At the entrance, we were searched and had to comply with the formalities, then the agents asked us frightful questions and sent us chilling looks that put us off.
There I met Emilio, who organised the courses and spoke Italian so flawlessly that I could not believe that he had learned it there. He had established the 'Fratelli Cervi' group and ran a well-stocked Italian bookshop.

Every year Franca Pesce, an Italian teacher from Turin, held Italian and Latin lectures there. She had trained Emilio, and Emilio had trained other people. Then the Institute of Culture, through its director Gianni Poma and Carmen Rosa, the other teacher, supported the project as well.

The students took the official examinations such as those held at the Institute and the University. I worked there for a couple of years; every Saturday I took a taxi and paid a visit to them.

At the end of the lesson, they used to take me to their cells and talk about the fight of the guerrilla groups during the dictatorship of Fujimori and their desire for a social change.

Most of the students belonged to the MRTA, the guerrilla Túpac Amaru group. Besides Emilio, there was Jaime Castillo Petruzzi, a Chilean boy, who had fought in Nicaragua.

Some days before returning to Italy, they invited me there and arranged for a surprise lunch. They prepared *papas a la huancaina*, *chicha morada*, *arroz con pollo*, *cabrito a la norteña*. My mouth still waters whenever I think about it! They did anything to make me happy, and I did it too to make them happy.

XXI. Otokongo

I had already decided to go back to Italy when one night, after the birthday of a friend of mine from Rome, I took a taxi at 11 p.m. The driver had a strange attitude.

I told him the address where I wanted to go, we agreed upon a price, and he started the engine. Suddenly I noticed that he took the wrong road, so I told him: «Excuse me, I'm not going there, but ... »

He turned to me with dreadful eyes, I did not know what was happening, I was breathless, he nodded and suddenly two hooded guys came out from the trunk and pointed a revolver at my chin! They started to scream madly.

«Shut up, bitch, or we'll kill you! Give us your wallet and credit card!»

My heart was in my mouth, I did not know whether to scream or die. The driver stared at me speechless.

«First we'll take the money and then we'll dismember you alive!»

I thought that they would take me to an ATM, but actually they left Lima and went to the suburban area.

«Aren't we going to get the money?» I asked.

«Shut up, bitch, or we'll kill you!»

After half an hour of threats and panic, we reached a house. My body moved autonomously, I could not control my stomach, my arms; I was writhing in pain.

«If you shout, you'll be dead, right?»
And he pointed a revolver at my temple.
The room was cold, I felt surrounded by human squalor. Six, seven people were waiting for us. Someone took out a bandage, while others blocked my hands, shoved me and laughed.
Oh my God, what were they going to do to me? I was like a bundle at the mercy of the waves; then they locked me in a room. Time seemed eternal and terror took hold of me. What if they dismembered me alive and sold my organs? What if I got raped by the fifteen of them? What if they emptied out my bank account? I did not know whether to shout or hope for a quick death. Time passed by but nothing happened.
Eventually, I called them and said that I wanted to stay with them; I would rather stay with my kidnapper than in the utmost solitude.
The boss had gone to the ATM to get money from my account and the others were getting bored. One of them was fucked up with psychotropic drugs: he was laughing and moving in a crazy way, he threatened me without any reason.
«I'll blow your brains out, you bitch, I'll put you to bed and fuck you until you die, then I'll throw you in a landfill.»
His voice made me shiver. His mood was going up and down, as a result of the drugs, I suppose. He pointed the

revolver at my temples, then he put it in his mouth. It was not easy to remain calm; I felt something between fear, anxiety and anger, I wanted to smash his face. However, I thought of the people who loved me and tried to keep my nerves under control.

Then one of them did not stop talking; I was pleased, because time passed more quickly, and I tried to examine the situation which obviously seemed to be out of my control.

I was still blindfolded and surrounded by the utmost darkness and he asked me a lot of things: «What is your favourite team? And how many languages can you speak? Do you like *ceviche*?»

To kill time, that guy decided to rape me but I literally overwhelmed him with words.

Suddenly the boss came back, that nice driver who had taken me there with his taxi. He said they would keep me there for some time, until they had decided what to do with me.

They could take five hundred euros a day from my credit card, and that sum was enough for them and the whole neighbourhood.

I listened to them in terror, I would have gone mad if I had stayed with them, so I said, «If I don't go home, my friend will go to the police.»

To reassure me, the boss replied: «Nobody will find you here,» and actually he was right.

I could not open my eyes, I could not cry, I could not go to the toilet, I could not move my hands, I could not lie on a bed, I could not do anything. The psychopath wanted to kill me, the boss wanted to bleed me, and the nice guy wanted to rape me. The latter was the best among them: he was kind, after all, so I talked softly to him.
«You've already taken my money, please, let me go! What if this happened to your sister ...»
«My sister wouldn't go out alone at night.»
Then the psychopath pointed the gun at my temple and said: «Kneel and don't move, we'll come back soon.»
When I lived in moments of panic I recall my childhood, the painting of Mariela (Maca'n), my father who used to take me to the seaside, a dear woman caressed my face.

Eventually, they came back: «We are going to set you free, bitch.»
What if they took me to a landfill to take my liver or kidneys and feed me to the dogs?
They violently dragged me back into the car, only insults and threats, one fondled me, the other kept a gun pointed at my chin and laughed. Its laughter was the most annoying thing.
An infinite journey towards freedom. We drove half an hour. I thought of Maca'n, when she came out of the stormy sea, and a starry night in Madrid. Evidently, they

had realised that I was terribly afraid of the landfill, since they repeated it all the time.
«We are going to leave you there, bitch.»
I saw myself surrounded by dogs. I figured out the news spread by the Italian newscasts, the family informed by the consul, and the friends crying along the street. Suddenly the car stopped.
«You're free, bitch. If you denounce us, we'll kill you.»
They left me in the middle of a highway, it was terribly cold, I took off the blindfold and started walking.
My stomach, liver and kidneys were hurting. I was paralysed and could not move my legs. Slowly, like a zombie, I reached a hotel. The light was on and some people were standing outside. I could not speak and I did not understand how I had survived.
«He ... he ... he ... » I could not even ask for help. They looked at me as if I were a junkie, everybody stood still.
«Call the po-po-lice, I want to go home.»
They called a taxi instead, and the driver was shocked as he saw me. «Oh my God, what happened to you?»
I could not even indicate my address. «Squa… square... but… excuse me, where are we now?»
«This is Otokongo Bridge, the bridge of freedom.»
He was very kind, but I feared that I could see again the face of the monster who had kidnapped me some hours earlier. It took me a long time to get rid of the nightmares.

Near home, I saw a police patrol and denounced the kidnapping. They drove me back home at seven a.m. and, when I opened the door, the alarm clock went off. I had to hold a lecture at the Institute of Culture. I had a shower: the water slid on my body. I lathered my tears, caressed the signs left by the ropes on my wrists, had a coffee and rushed to work.

XXII. Temblor

It was 15thAugust 2007 and I was at the Institute of Italian Culture, in Avenida Arequipa in Lima. In the southern hemisphere, it is winter in August, so I could not sunbathe. It was about 7 p.m., I was writing some words on the blackboard with a marker, when I suddenly heard some noises: pa-pa-pa-pa-pa! It sounded like a machine gun shooting at the windows. Pa-pa-pa-pa! I looked upwards and saw that the chandelier was swinging, the tables began to stagger; I stared at the students' eyes.

«Temblor, temblor!» we all shouted.

We tried to get out, but the door did not open, we felt like a boat in the middle of the sea. Desperate cries came from the first and second floor, the stairs moved like a raft.

«Temblor, temblor!»

We gathered in the hall and saw the building stumbling around us. I hugged Javier and Rosa, two of my dearest colleagues, but the powerful quakes pushed us down on our knees.

«Ave María purisima!»

We looked at each other in terror and thought that we were going to die.

The earthquake lasted three eternal minutes, it was as if the earth were roaring and about to swallow us. Javier was

holding me tight and I was thinking of Maca'n who was somewhere out there.
Five hundred deaths and thousands injured in less than three minutes, the epicentre was Chincha. 7.9 on the Richter scale. There were holes in the streets like cracks in the middle of the sea.
As soon as the panic was over, I rushed to the avenue and took the first taxi I saw.
In Breña, where Maca'n lived, the electricity went out, people were walking like zombies in the empty city. I came home and knocked furiously at the door: Maca'n opened the door and we hugged. Then we found Loki and Blanqui, a dalmatian and a cocker, running wildly in the garden. We had survived, but there had been so many deaths in those three endless minutes of terror.
My fortieth birthday would be the following week, and I wanted to organise a big party. A celebration of life among the ruins of death.

XXIII. Fiesta

For my fortieth birthday, Annarita hosted us in her attic on the 16th floor of a building in Miraflores, and the Italian community moved there. Everybody was there: Giovanni, the consul, my colleagues of the University, the Institute of Culture and the Italian High School, a lot of students and the friends of mine from Lima. Paolo, Corona, Maite, Jaime, Jorge, Marcello, Patrizia, John, Cesare, Chiqui, Iris. In the background we could enjoy a wonderful view of the ocean and the skyscrapers of the city: the party was wonderful. Someone brought some food, others improvised a theatre show, others sang the opera. We were surrounded by a swimming pool, the squash courts, the generosity of Annarita and the embrace of Corona. At the party there was also my teacher of martial arts, the lady who used to prepare my coffee, Jean Pierre from the French embassy and Pablo who had just got out of prison.

Their looks accompanied me around the world, and now that I'm living in Moscow, I take them with me to the Kremlin, on the Red Square, in the house/shelter of Majakovsky. At night, I hug them gripping the pillow tightly. I feel them inside of me and I want them to remain there forever.

BRIDGE

I. Potosì

After so many travels in Europe, I decided to move to the south of the world, and I thought of a bridge able to symbolically join Madrid (where I was at that moment) and Potosì.

I had learnt about the bridge some years before while I was in Madrid; in a room that smelled like love, I was reading *Open Veins of Latin America* by Eduardo Galeano. That bridge was made of gold and silver, but also of the bones of six million natives who died in Cerro Rico exploited by the European and Latin-American ruling classes who wanted to become richer and richer.

I became familiar with Madrid, I knew its magnificence and its decadence; I spent many afternoons in front of El Escorial and I used to get lost in the alleys of El Rastro between Chueca, Malasaña, El Retiro and Lavapiés; I admired the paintings by Miro and Goya, I drank amazing coffee in the Santa Isabel film library and smoked Like strike at La Lupe in Calle de la Torrecilla del Leal.

But I did not know where Potosì was, until one day I found out that it was in Bolivia, between Sucre, Uyuni, La Paz and Tarija. The exploitation of that immense mountain of copper, tin, nickel and silver had been so reckless that Cerro Rico, once majestically stretching towards the

clouds, had been lowered by hundreds of meters, thus changing the lunar and rural landscape.
I was told that by a man who pointed at the mountain: «Do you see those houses over there? It was impossible to see them before, because they were covered by the top of the greatest silver mine in the world. The Spaniards had devastated it, and left us in hunger, misery and desperation.»
The plunder perpetrated by the Spaniards was so extensive that the Government of Madrid had signed an agreement which granted a visa to every Bolivian who wanted to live in Europe; as a consequence, many Andean people declared that they had born in Sucre or Cochabamba or in Guayaquil or Arequipa in order to find love and freedom far from their native countries. When everything went right, nobody noticed anything, and Peruvians and Ecuadorians returned back home as Bolivians in disguise, but when they needed a document attesting to their marital or financial status, they realised that their *Mattia Pascal* did not exist and their dream of freedom withered away. They wanted to go back home, see their friends and family, but they were imprisoned as soon as they landed in overseas airports, and were accused of the worst crime, namely the betrayal of their country. The bridge in front of them was not covered with gold but rather with thorns.
I thought of those six million natives killed by whiskey and coca leaves to withstand temperatures of fifty above

and below zero; they used to drink, smoke, run up debts, and were buried alive in the mines for months, losing their mind, sleep, appetite, sight and health; as soon as they saw their children and relatives again, they could not even speak, because the mines had taken away their soul. They were so ashamed of their condition that they just wanted to descend once again into the bowels of the Earth.

In the mines women gave birth to their children and men buried their comrades, the children learned to read and write, and the Church made money with the 'tithe' on slavery. Bones were piled up in every corner of the mine, there were neither crosses nor graves for the corpses; in the subsoil of one of the richest and most fascinating regions in the world, there was just hunger, misery and despair.

In the 17th century, Potosì had more inhabitants than Paris and London, it was the third most densely populated city in the world; nowadays, in the 21st century, it is a sad and abandoned city, poor and bare; the Spaniards took away everything, even some statues covered with gold and silver, and today the city is visited by emotionless tourists who get in touch with the most authentic memory of poverty in the south of the world.

I wanted to go to Potosì, I wanted to tear the bridge made of human bones into pieces, I wanted to raise my voice to condemn those events which made humanity slave to its hunger for conquest, I wanted to spend one day in that mine to understand how it feels to live down there, for decades, without being caressed by the sunlight.

One year after my arrival in South America, in 2003, I was about to live one of the most terrifying experiences of my whole life: I was going to spend one day in the Potosì mine.

I went there by bus from Cuzco and asked a guy to guide me there.

«You don't need to go down there,» he said «but if you decide to descend, avoid any panic attacks, because in few minutes there will be hundreds of thousands of tonnes of earth above us. This is a journey to the bowels of hell.»

As soon as he uttered these words, I was already losing my nerve, but I decided to continue. I curse my height (5.5 feet), I bent my head but I soon had to bend my knees and use my elbows to drag myself forward.

I was sweating like a horse, then I entered some small recesses that looked like ovens. I tried to take off my scarf and jacket, but I could not move, since the space was too narrow; subsequently, I reached another recess where the temperature was ten degrees lower and the sweat froze on my skin. Everything around me was dark, only a small lantern placed on my helmet lit up the path. Then I started to feel hungry, thirsty, sleepy and tired; my body, squeezed in a camouflage suit, was drawing this to my attention.

My guide noticed that I was blue in the face: «Do you already need to chew coke? Let's go on a few metres and look for a comfortable place to have a rest.»
I looked at my watch and asked: «How long have we been here?»
«Less than half an hour, we must stay here until evening.»
I was relieved by the idea that outside there were the sun, the light and the stars, but panic made me think that I might spend the rest of my life in that hell. «Will we survive?»
He smiled. «The first hours are the hardest, then the body gets used to this environment.»
«*Good God,*» I thought «*Why in God's name did I do this!?Why in God's name did I read Marx when I was just fourteen?*»
Obviously, I feared that the mountain might crumble, and we might get locked there forever. Who would descend there to recover our bodies? Would they care about me with so many dead men buried down there?
We reached a sort of room. There were five or six miners with a blank expression, but as soon as they saw a woman, they behaved kindly, as if we had met at an elegant party. They let me sit down, cleaned a bottle with the palm of their hand and gave it to me.
«Drink, it will do you good ...»
It was pure alcohol, eighteen degrees.
«No thanks,» I replied «I don't drink alcohol.»

«You don't drink alcohol? Here you can't bear the heat, you can't bear the cold, you can't bear anything except for whiskey and coke. If you take it, you'll be able to get out of here, otherwise you'll go crazy.»

I eventually took their advice and, after some rest, I continued to walk. My veins were exploding and suddenly I heard a roar that reminded me of an earthquake ...

Oh my God, what's happening?

My guide assured me: «Probably some miner has blown up a rock with dynamite to clear a path, otherwise we wouldn't have been able to descend down here. Originally it was a mountain, not a highway!»

«Oh my God! Dynamite. Just what I needed, damned Marx. Now I could have been comfortably sunbathing on the beach instead of descending into this hell to try to find the secret of our wealth! I reject the privileges of my class, but I don't want to die under these ruins, so please, take me away from here!»

My elbows were bruised, I could no longer chew coke, my mind was blurry, I just wanted a hot shower and a warm dinner.

«Is it a long way to go?» I asked.

«We are climbing Cerro, but here the road is closed and we must bypass the obstacle; come on, in few hours we'll see the stars again, are you still having panic attacks?»

The coke had benumbed my cheekbones: I sometimes touched my cheeks to make sure they were still there. Yes,

they still existed, but I was looking forward to resuming my usual life.
Suddenly I saw a light in the dark: I did not know if it was a hallucination or if we were really getting out of the tunnel. I started to slowly stretch my knees, then my wrists and neck, until eventually I saw a wooden door. «Is this the exit?»
The guy nodded, and I was so happy that I almost tore apart the camouflage suit that had stuck to my body.

The sky was beautiful, the stars were beautiful, the breeze that caressed my cheeks was beautiful. I had gotten out of the mine, and I was happy, because I had dedicated one day of my life to the amazing *Cerro* Potosí, *cerro* which reminded me of that *calle Cabeza* in Madrid, number thirty-three where I found *Open veins of Latin America* by Eduardo Galeano on a bed that smelled of love. A legendary book, a legendary love story.

II. Maca’n

Maca'n was waiting for me outside the mine, and we decided to visit together Sucre, the capital of Bolivia, and then the largest and most fascinating *salar* in the world, Salar de Uyuni. We had learnt about an area of five hundred kilometres covered with salt, statues made of salt, cities, hotels and houses entirely covered with salt. If you touched the soil and put your finger into the mouth, you could taste salt; swans and flamingos flew over big lakes surrounded by salt; you could even drive on kilometres of salted surfaces with the jeep. If I had not gone there and had just seen some pictures of that scenery, I would have thought that it was a lunar landscape, while actually it is the south of the world, where fantasy and reality combine in horizons covered with salt.

Maca'n had brought along her works and set-up improvised 'callejeras'[20] exhibitions before the intrigued passers-by and the fascinated natives, who were attracted by her apparent almond-eyes Japanese girl look that was part of their culture. As already stated, I met Maca'n in Cuzco and we decided to travel together to the south of the world; after Uyuni we headed to Mendosa, Cordova, Santa Fe, Rosario and eventually to Buenos Aires to claim,

---

[20]Alomg the streets.

together with the mothers, the body of the young who had disappeared during the dictatorship of Videla. After Argentina, we visited Chile led by Victor Jara, Uruguay with its Tupamaros and Paraguay with the opponents to Stroessner.

Maca'n felt the revolution inside her; she was always ready to put her rebel-like poncho on and fight for her people. One day, on a Saturday afternoon, I met her in the Andes at a meeting of 'campesinos'[21]. With her blue braids, she protested so that the native languages, Quechua and Aymara, were regarded as official in the public schools of the country.

Maca'n struggled against the government which forced the people, even in remote villages, to speak a language introduced by the conquerors and rejected by the local populations.

«We want to break the chains that bind us to the oppressors, because we are rebels, we are proud of our culture and we are the creators of our history,» she used to say.

And then she took me along the streets of Cuzco, among the ruins of the sacred valley.

«Here there was the greatest temple of our Incan culture, Coricancha, the temple of the Sun, which is named after

---

[21]Peasants.

its walls that were entirely covered with gold and shone in the sunlight».

Then she smiled and continued her speech: «It had belonged to our land until the Spaniards plundered it and took away those precious sheets on their big ships. Now it is as bare as our soul ... may those bastards be cursed forever!»

And then I met her in Lima on the occasion of a protest against Fujimori, who was arrested by the Interpol in Chile. The far-left movements asked for his extradition, they wanted him - who had hundreds of thousands of regime opponents massacred by death squads - to be judged in his country.

A lot of people had gathered in front of the Chilean embassy; on one side of the road there were the supporters of the dictatorship, on the other side there were those who defended social freedoms and civil rights, led by Maca'n.

Maca'n shouted slogans supporting freedom through a megaphone and asked for the extradition of a man who had killed nine students and one professor at La Cantuta University and was also responsible for the Barrios Altos[22] massacre, as well as another massacre of thousands *campesinos* in the forest.

---

[22] The Barrios Altos massacre is one of the worst crimes committed by the Colina Group in Lima on 3 November 1991, at night. 15 people were killed - eight men, three women and a 9 year-old child – who were charged with the collection of money for Sendero Luminoso. It has never been established whether they were actually members or supporters of this movement.

The supporters of the dictatorship screamed madly, and suddenly the police used irritating tear gas to disperse the protesters. Maca'n was intoxicated by the gas, but soon recovered her strength and was ready to confront the fierce supporters of the dictatorship, «Please, Maca'n, stop or they'll kill you.»

Then she rushed to a banner, grabbed it, threw it on the ground and screamed: «You bastard Fascists, go to hell!»

The policemen were about to assault her, «Run away, Maca'n, don't stop!»; she ran away through the crowd, then she turned and screamed from a distance «Down with Fujimori!»

I still remember her on a Thursday afternoon with the mothers who were protesting on the square: she held a banner and shouted: «*Ni un paso atrás*!»[23]"; she marched like a soldier and looked like a little Frida with those markers that came out of her ears and with her hands stained with paint, ink and passion.

The Argentinian government wanted to compensate those mothers whose children had been taken away, but they did not want any money, they claimed back the blood that had been drained from their veins.

Maca'n was there with them and used to read, under the trees of the San Telmo Grafitis park, a famous story

---

[23]Not one step back!

written by Julio Cortázar[24] which dealt with two young people who had fallen in love during the dictatorship; then she went out at night to paint the streets of the city recalling a revolution about which many people had dreamed.

And when soldiers on horseback came to repress the protest of the mothers, Maca'n raised her arms up high and used her markers to paint the revolt of her youth on the soldier's faces.

«No, Maca'n, they will really kill you!»

And while they were dragging her towards the Santiago Stadium, she sang with Victor Jara and Silvio Rodriguez: «*Ojala que las hojas no te toquen el cuerpo cuando caigan!*» Please Maca'n, don't provoke them, «*Para que no las puedas convertir en cristal!*» Maca'n, hold on, cry:«*Ojala que la lluvia deje de ser el milagro que baja por tu cuerpo.*» Sooner or later we will set you all free «*Ojala que la luna pueda salir sin ti, ojalá, ojalá, ojalá…*[25]»

[24] Julio Cortázar (Brussels, 26 August 1914 - Paris, 12 February 1984) was an Argentinian writer, poet, literary critic, essayist and playwright who acquired French citizenship. He was the master of short stories, especially fantasy, metaphysical and mystery ones.

[25] Ojala, a song by Silvio Rodriguez, a Cuban singer, which is dedicated to Augusto Pinochet, author of the coup in Chile on 11 September 1973, which overthrew the socialist government of Salvator Allende. This song represents the protest against every dictatorship all over the world.

In those years rebellions also broke out in the Andean forest. In Peru there were the MRTA, Sendero, the paramilitary groups, the Colina Group; the victims of the conflict were sixty-nine thousand, and deeply shocked the population.

I knew little of this when I was asked to work at the Peruvian universities; I was offered chairs in Lima, Cuzco, Tumbes, Huacho, Ayacucho and Iquitos; so I bought a one-way ticket from Europe to the south of the world. I was travelling with Maca'n to the most remote locations of the continent, when one day I decided to move from the Cuzco to the Lima University, thereafter we left Montevideo and headed to Chaco, and then to Santa Cruz, Cochabamba, La Paz, Ayacucho, Arequipa and then again to Lima. The capital of the Spanish *Virreinato* was a beautiful city, with an amazing old town and the breath-taking Plaza de Armas. The cathedral was the burial place of Pizarro, the symbol of a power which had plundered and devastated a continent.

«A murderer is buried there,» Maca'n said smiling at me, «But sooner or later we'll blow him up in his grave.»

III. La Cantuta

When I was told that I would hold lectures at La Cantuta University in Lima, I was happy and proud of holding my courses at the University which embodied the students' revolts and still nourished rebellion. I made an appointment with the directors of the department and moved from Lima to Chosica; it was about thirty miles as the crow flies, however, in a city with ten million citizens without the subway, it might take two or three hours depending on the traffic. When I got off of the bus, I found myself in a sunny village; we had to reach the middle of the track and then take a taxi, because the road that led to the university was not paved. I gradually saw a large fenced green area which was the campus: it took half a day to cross it, so I used to call the various departments to inform them of my arrival as soon as I got there. Then I watched the llamas crouched on the grass: I approached them fearing that they might spit at me, but fortunately they never did.

The fame of the La Cantuta students was justified; every day they occupied a canteen, a library, or a study room; as I moved from one department to another, I often heard their slogans. I recognised the voice of Patty, John, Rosa, Claudio and Pamela. They never backed down in spite of the arrests and the clubs, but they always grew stronger and fiercer. They seemed to have nine lives like cats. Then they entered the classrooms while I was holding a lecture. «Professor,» they asked me «May we read a declaration?» They summoned a meeting or an assembly, I do not know how they could manage so many activities; my colleagues shunned them. «These guys just stir up trouble»; well, I was precisely looking for that trouble.

The successors of Cesar Vallejo[26] were referred to as 'Amauta' and used to keep a clock with the image of Mariategui[27]at their headquarters, which beat to the time of their protests. They were hindered by the dean.

«Professor, would you mind asking for the projector? We would like to watch a film on El Che's guerrilla.»

Avec plaisir[28], guys!

One day they told me that they were going to Lima to take part in a demonstration against the TLC (Free Trade Agreement) with the United States, which the Peruvian government was about to sign.

«Be careful guys, they'll beat you up.» I had just held a lesson in the afternoon, then I took a taxi to go back home to the centre of Lima.

---

[26]César Abraham Vallejo Mendoza (Santiago de Chuco, 16 March 1892 – Paris, 15 April 1938) was a Peruvian poet.

[27]José Carlos Mariátegui La Chira (Moquegua, 14 June 1894 - Lima, 16 April 1930) was a Peruvian journalist, sociologist and politician. Also called Amauta, he is regarded as one of the first and most important Marxist thinkers of Latin America.

[28]Gladly.

We were stuck in the traffic and the smoke of tear gas could be distinguished from the buildings; I got off the taxi and walked home. However, there was a checkpoint on the street and I saw people running everywhere.
Eventually, I opened the door of the house and prepared myself for the worst; the phone did not ring, but I was not calm anyway. I switched on the TV and watched the images of the revolt: they reminded me of Genoa 2001 and I started to fear for the safety of those guys; at 3 in the morning I was woken up by the ringing of the phone: it was John.
«Professor, they've wiped us out, pushed us into a street with no exit and beat us up. Now we are at the central police station, we need a doctor, we can't even breathe; they told us that we could call a lawyer and we thought of you. Excuse me if I have bothered you, but we don't know what to do.»
«How many of you are there?»
«Seven. We have been accused of incitement of terrorism, because we had a flyer of the trade unions. Pamela had a panic attack, she is nineteen years old, it was the first time that she protested with us along the streets.»
«Stay there, I'll come.»
I got dressed in two minutes and rushed to them. Outside the police station, there were some lawyers who were always ready to assist any customer. I talked to one of

them and we agreed upon the price. «We must help them get out of there,» I told him «They're very young.»
The lawyer was skilful; I went to the policemen and told them that I had come to set my students free in the name of the university at which I worked. The policemen looked at me amazed:«*Are you a professor?*» And as soon as they checked my credentials, they almost fainted.
They did not know whether they could release the students; a girl had bruises on her neck, John had injuries on his head, Patty had a dislocated arm, and all of them had lung problems. It was early in the morning, so I called the dean who was getting ready for work.
«Hello Manuel,» I said, «Excuse me, I hope you don't mind me calling this early. Seven students of ours have been arrested and illegally kept in prison. The police commissioner wants to talk to you; please, help them.»
The dean was a fascist, but when I said «seven students of ours», I evidently played on his feelings. Obviously, he supported the TLC or had no opinion about it, however he fiercely faced the commissioner to my great surprise
«OK, now we'll sign the documents and the students will be set free. Yes, they're fine. They just have some bruises, probably from where they have fallen. Thank you, dean.»
Thus the commissioner ordered the policemen to release the students and we eventually left that place of torture.
«What are we going to do now, professor?»
«How about having breakfast?»

They had many wounds and were sleepy, however they were happy. Blessed youth!

I went back home and they took a bus to the university; we met later in the afternoon on the occasion of my lesson at the campus. I knew they would come to me, so I talked about them to the other students who attended my course. The lesson dealt with the TLC, repression and the rights both of the demonstrators and of the people arrested.

Then the students fuelled an intense debate: according to them, the world needed a change, however, when someone tried to improve our conditions, we were often distracted or just looked away.

And when the seven arrested students opened the door – some bandaged, some with bruises and clear signs of violence –we were all moved and my students stood up and welcomed them with a long applause.

It was a magical moment. I was proud of those guys who had risked their lives to defend an idea; I felt the energy of their youth, the strength of their ideas, the passion with which they defended their lifestyle. They were battered, but they were still alive, which should not be taken for granted in the south of the world.

The nine students and the professor who had been kidnapped in the night by the Colina Group death squads had not been so lucky. They were taken away on 18 July 1992, after Fujimori's coup. They were accused of incitement of terrorism and then were taken to the countryside, where they were tortured. Bruises, injuries. The guys had nothing to confess, therefore the torturers were upset. They took some shovels from the hoods of their cars.

«Now dig your own graves,» they said and the students were forced to do this under the threat of guns. As soon as they had finished, they were hit at the back of their head, pum-pam-pam!

They remained in those graves for years, and when their mothers called for justice, the government replied: «Your children are in the forest with the guerrillas.»

Justice was never done, but one night a vagabond fell asleep precisely on that hill, where the corpses of those innocent people were buried, and saw fingers emerging under a bush, then an arm, a hand, a rib. The man got scared and called a journalist.

The country was still led by Fujimori. «We'll investigate this case,» he said, but everyone knew that he would cover up the evidence.

Now, twenty years after that terrible massacre, the dictator is serving the sentence, as he could not benefit from the pardons and amnesties granted to the torturers of the Barrios Altos and La Cantuta victims. He will never give us back the corpses of the nine students and the professor, or of the youth killed in the *pollada* of Barrios Altos, however he is not leading a joyful life in prison, at least.

Alberto Fujimori is deprived of his freedom, as he deprived many people of it during his ten-years' regime. It is easy to rule in a palace, but it is difficult to do it in prison.

In the evening, I left the llamas behind me and while I was driving home with my taxi, I thought of those guys woken up suddenly in the middle of the night: Hugo, Manuel, Dora, Luis, Robert, Armando, Felipe, Bertila, Juan, Pablo who could not even hug their parents and friends for the last time. Therefore, when my students stood up in front of the young rebels who had fought against the TLC, I was proud of them: they stood up and applauded, and I joined them.

IV. Cuzco

Once in Cuzco, I spent the afternoons in the sacred valley between the Inca ruins of Ollantaytambo, Tipón, Saxawaman, Aguas Calientes and Machu Picchu.

I cannot describe the emotions that I felt whenever I opened the window of my bedroom and saw, in the distance, the green and majestic Andes. I used to live near Coricancha - the golden temple devoted to the gods which was wildly devastated by the Spaniards - between Plaza de Armas and the Saint Anthony University, where I taught Italian on the rainy afternoons of a summer still to be discovered. I had never lived at a height of four thousand metres; as soon as I arrived in Cuzco, I realised that I could hardly breathe: I could not walk, go up the stairs, I could not even finish those fine cigarettes that I used to smoke during the day. I feared that I was about to die, so I sucked the air of that Andean space which took me closer to the clouds, the curses against the rain and tobacco, the willingness to give up bad habits, aware of the fact that everything can be given up, except for passions.

During the first few days, I felt the blood flowing in my veins like a river in full spate; I used to chew many coke leaves until I went numb and I could certainly not hold my lessons at the university under those conditions. I could not speak, I could not smile, I could not move any muscle;

‘Soroche’[29] is the name which refers to this feeling. Only those who have lived this experience know what I mean. Then, I gradually started to react; at night, my ribs pushed upward and the pieces of my chest dislocated due to the martial arts beginning to fit again. The pain was unbearable, my bones cracked at night and I could hear crick-crack, I kept chewing coke, crick-crack, then woke up, had a coffee and went to the university.

In Cuzco I lived in a '*posada*', which is a large farmhouse with wooden stairs, chairs, counters and a roof; downstairs there was a restaurant, while the first floor, where I lived, hosted the rooms for the guests.
That place was attended both by tourists and by the local citizens; we were surrounded by the Andean culture and it felt like an eternal journey.
In the morning I met my students, who enjoyed our meeting in front of a fish soup or a ‘*cabrito*’[30] instead of those boring coffee machine sin the dreary classrooms. They talked to me about their personal choices, and then in the evening we used to go together to the disco or have a walkalong the alleys that flanked the Andes.

---

[29]The word '*soroche*' refers to the 'altitude sickness' which affects most of the tourists who visit Peru. Greater fatigue, general weakness, headache, nausea and tachycardia are the most common symptoms observed in the first days of stay at altitudes above 1,500 m a.s.l. They are normal reactions of the organism and generally disappear after few days.
[30] Kid.

However, I was so focused on my lesson on Calvino and Manzoni that I sometimes forgot how people still died of cold and hunger in spite of all the local wealth.
We could not stop it happening and did whatever we could; for example, when I went on holidays one week a month or one month per year, I left the keys to my apartment to some students. «Do whatever you want: you're free and freedom must be exercised.»
I took part in wonderful excursions in Machu Picchu with some students of mine; some of them talked about history, others of literature, others asked me to climb the Huayna Picchu, on the nose of the Inca full of cliffs.
Life in Cuzco was totally wild, and whenever I left the campus after a day of work, that fresh Andean air purified my mind and soul.

One day I was called by the Italian Embassy and was told about Vittoria; I already knew that there was an Italian woman in Cuzco who had carried out amazing projects, however I had not met her yet; so I eventually got her telephone number and called her.
On a Sunday afternoon I took a taxi to Avenida Argentina to meet her. I was welcomed by a good-looking, white-haired woman with a bright smile.
Vittoria was about eighty years old, she was a retired maths teacher from Turin and came the Andean region for the first time a few years earlier to carry out a project

promoted by a small association with the purpose of repairing the damage of the civil war.
Then they ran out of money and everyone had returned home, except for her.
Vittoria had given up on Italy and Europe; she invested her pension in the construction of a house, followed by another one, where she hosted girls and women raped by life and love.
These women ranged from eight months to sixty years old; they had been abandoned by their families who did not know how to sustain them, therefore they were 'sold' and enslaved by other families who entrusted them with the humblest jobs and deprived them of wages and education; they were often mistreated, raped and abused in endless ways.
When these girls got pregnant or revolted, they were banished from the houses that had welcomed them and did not know where to go. They could neither return to their original families - who could not re-admit them in those conditions –nor look at the future, because they had no money, no education, they did not even know the country where they lived.
Where could they go to, then?
They applied to Vittoria, of course!
As soon as I entered that house, I felt like I was in a large gynaecium. There were women of all ages and colours; there bore the signs of pain, but also of the dignity of those

who had been saved from the gallows and did not want to turn back.

Girls raped and tortured for years by men fifty years older than them, forced to become mothers without having been daughters, and Vittoria welcomed them and lived with them.

She had arranged for autonomous schools, where volunteers from all over the world held lessons to those girls: they taught them how to play with a ball and take pictures; moreover, they studied Quechua and also English, French and art history.

«What can I do for you, Vittoria?» I asked.

«To earn some money, we have built a B&B here in the Andes; it is attended by tourists from all over the world, but especially from Italy. I can't speak Italian with the girls; considering that you hold lessons at the university, can you help them with some scholarships?»

No sooner said than done. I called the Embassy to submit a small cultural integration project, and in few days scholarships were granted to all the girls of Vittoria's associations.

I was so happy to see them in the classrooms! From the torturers of the upper classes of Cuzco to the university, where they could dream of a better future, at least.

However, I could not understand how parents, albeit poor and uneducated, could get rid of their daughter, their own flesh and bones, in the hope that these girls might lead a different life with 'rich' people (with reference only to material wealth.)

Poverty is awful, those who have not experienced it cannot understand what it means, however these girls were denied the opportunity to go back, to re-join their families, who still preferred to keep them away instead of welcoming them back home with the signs of sin on their body.

This is what happened to many women in the world, from the Andes to the Pyrenees, from Bolivia to China ... the girls mistreated by everyone - especially by their mothers –end up pleasing everyone, except for themselves.

«Do you see that girl?» Vittoria asked me one day. «As she was just twelve years old, she was left alone with a man aged eighty; she had been raped, tortured and forced to kill her own children.»

«Kill her children?»

«Yes. As soon as she gave birth to a child, she was forced to kill him by drowning him in buckets filled with dirty water. Her body had to be always ready for a new pregnancy. The old man and his daughters witnessed these atrocities: they thought that they had bought the girl at the cattle market.

One day she could not resist any longer and flew away; the social workers took her: she was totally distressed. The other girls treated her. Here the mother's day is a sad day. Nobody wants to celebrate the woman who brought them into the world.»

V. Castro Castro

One day, at the Institute of Italian Culture in Lima, Carmen Rosa - a colleague of mine - stopped me in the corridor and asked: «Did you know that the university has signed an agreement with Castro Castro, the high-security prison in Lima?»

«An agreement? And what does prison have to do with us?»

«We may hold lessons to the prisoners instead of the students of the upper and middle class families of Lima,»

«That's amazing! I'm looking forward to starting this activity! I'll check my agenda.»

I was so excited and happy! Although in Lima I held lessons at the University, at the Institute of Culture, at the Antonio Raimondi Italian High School as well as to the nurses in a hospital for anorexic and bulimic girls, I immediately seized the opportunity to hold lessons in the prison with all my energy.

As soon as I indicated my willingness to participate in this project, on Saturday afternoon, between a lesson at the Italian Institute of Culture and a martial arts session, I was called by Carlos Alvares who worked for the *Dignità umana* NGO, dealing with the supply of language courses to the prisons of the country. He picked me up at the Institute at one p.m. and then we drove together to Castro

Castro. We had a document signed by the NGO and the Italian Embassy, moreover we had all the permits required, however our admission into the prison was not certain.
«But why?» I asked Carlos.
«There is no reason, you must do what they decide.»
Many people had gathered in front of the prison: it looked like a fair! These women were waiting to see their dear ones. They cast intrigued glances at me, probably because I was a European woman, and also due to what I was wearing.
Carlos noticed that they were interested in me and said: «According to an internal circular, women must wear a skirt, did you know this?»
«That's ridiculous!»
«They wouldn’t agree with you. Most of them have been here for fifteen, twenty years and want women to be as feminine as possible; if they protest, I’ll try to persuade them to let you enter».
“*Good start!*” I thought.
When they stopped us, they immediately pointed out my clothes. I pretended not to notice their remarks, but then they asked me why I wanted to teach the prisoners instead of children, who had not killed anyone. I kept quite to avoid further conflicts; obviously, they wanted to isolate the prisoners, they did not want them to enter into contact with us and, above all, they did not want them to learn other languages possibly useful outside the prison.

According to a decree, the education/penalty reduction ratio expressed in years was seven to one. Seven years of study for a penalty reduction of one year: it was not a great achievement, but at least it was a hope to which the prisoners could cling.
In the State prison of Peru, many lessons were held: English, French, Quechua, Italian, Latin, drawing, mathematics, ceramics, astronomy, and physics. Everyone contributed to this project.

The French group, based on its Foucaultian tradition, was a pioneer in the teaching activity. Not only did it supply teachers, but it even paid them and, once the penalty was served, looked for a job for the former prisoners.
Italy was bringing up in the rear, as often happens in these cases: in fact, the Italian teachers were not paid and were even mocked by their colleagues.
«Aren't you afraid of teaching guerrillas?»
«Well, actually I'm more afraid of you!»
Every time I held my lessons in the prison, I was subjected to absurd cheks: a policewoman checked even my bra and had such an arrogant attitude, that I thought: "*Why in God's name did I do that!?*"
A series of bars, gates, keys that opened and closed doors, and, eventually, the smile of Jaime, Emilio, as well as of the other prisoners who were waiting for me to start their Italian lesson.

Emilio spoke Italian flawlessly; I wondered where hecame from, but he told me that he had learned Italian in prison thanks to some volunteers ... congratulations! And now, it was his turn to teach the others.
«That's the way it goes, isn't it?»he asked.
«Yes, but it's a jungle out there, Emilio.»
We used to teach grammar and conversation and read something together; one day I told them that I was drawing up some tests.
«Tests?» they asked in a shocked tone.
«May we copy? And if we don't pass them, will we have a second chance?»
They looked like frightened kids rather than armed guerrillas. Sometimes life is really strange.

I used to spend the whole afternoon with them and then, at the end of the lessons, Emilio or Jaime offered me a coffee in their cell.
The first time I asked them if we were allowed to meet there.
«Of course! We are free here!»
I laid down on their beds and we talked about the reasons that had led them to shoulder a gun and fight.
«We had no choice,» they replied. «There was the dictatorship of Belaunde, of Alan García, of Fujimori, and how could we fight against the people's ignorance? In this country, if you are rich, you are regarded as a 'God', but if

you are poor, you are worthless. Without money you can't have food, education and healthcare; is it worth living a life like that? Slaving away all day long?»
«I was charged with kidnappings» Jaime said «And we needed money to be invested in education. The MRTA members were Guevarists; I came from Chile, from MIR, Movimiento de Izquierda Revolucionaria, and had already fought in Nicaragua. As stated by El Che, we wanted to fight everywhere in the world, we were willing to give our life for the revolution. Then we were caught; we are political prisoners and they treat us like dirt, but we don't give up.»
The cell was full of posters, books written in Quechua, English and French.
«I lived in Paris, too,» he said. «After the coup in Chile, we decided to return here, because so many people needed our help. We could seek political asylum and remain in France, but this was not what we wanted. I spent wonderful years in Nicaragua, we won in spite of the Contras[31], but we could not stay there. In Peru there was still the dictatorship, the people rose up in the forest and in the countryside; the MRTA needed our help, and I could not look away. Now I have a partner in Lima and we have two children; I want to get out of here, because this world still needs us.»

---

[31]The *contras* are counter-revolutionary Nicaraguan armed groups.

A siren interrupted our conversation.
«Now you must go to Isabella, otherwise you'll get stuck here.»

I was looking for Emilio who took me to the checkpoints. He used a public telephone and we often spent the whole night talking.
«Emilio, I must go to sleep now, tomorrow I'm holding lectures at the university.»
«I'm so jealous! Good night and have a nice day at work, Isabella *querida*.»

When I decided to return to Europe, I wondered: "*How will I tell this to the students?*"
My students, my guerrillas, would suffer very much from our separation. I communicated my decision at the beginning of my lesson. They did not want to cry, so they arranged for a lavish lunch; they prepared a lot of tasty dishes: *chicha morada*, *papas a la huancaina*, *cabrito* a la *norteña, ceviche con limón.*
That day I asked for the permission to bring along a camera and we had so much fun as if we were on holidays in Hawaii! The prison director wanted to see the photos: he checked them all, also because he feared that I could send the newspapers the photos of some prisoners who were going on hunger strike and had sewn their mouths shut with a needle and thread.

Antauro was one of them: he was the brother of former President Ollanta Humala, who had arranged for a coup against the government of Alejandro Toledo. His look shocked me; I looked at his sewn lips and felt a deep pain that pierced my stomach.

I had a great lunch with my students: we listened to music and danced until late afternoon. At seven p.m.it all ended and the curtain dropped; I had to go, otherwise I would stay there with them, forever. I tore my heart out of my chest and left it behind the bars, then I saw my body move towards the cells, leave them behind, close a door, open another door, get on a taxi, wipe my tears, return to Lima, take a plane and finally arrive in Europe.
When my heart joined my body once again, I felt all those guys inside me: I could feel their smiles, their fears, I brought them along on the streets of the world and I felt free and happy like never before.

VI. La Higuera

One day I was in Santa Cruz, a wonderful city north-east of Bolivia, when I bumped into a demonstration of students in a square. I had already seen that scene before in many parts of the world, but that demonstration was special. The images of El Che stood out against the landscape; if I had ignored history, I would have wondered if he had been just killed in the Andes. Everybody, even the youngest guys, bore something that recalled him: a pin, a flyer, a poster to be waved in the wind.

«What's happening?» I asked «Why are there so many pictures of El Che?»

«He was killed right here, in our forest. Don't you know?»

Darn, that's it! When I lived in Europe, the Bolivian forest seemed a place out of reach, but now, after a long journey, I had eventually reached it.

«He was shot by the Americans there, at the end of that valley.»

«How do I get there?» I asked.

«Well, you have to go to Cochabamba, stop in Samaipata, take a bus to the great valley and then get on a truck to La Higuera.»

«Thank you, I'll start my journey.»

As soon as I arrived in Samaipata, I realised that I had just a few dollars, so I wanted to withdraw some cash at an

ATM, but I had left the civilisation behind and there was no bank within two hundred kilometres.

Good God, what will I do now? I was in a panic, while the others were calmer.

«There are no banks here, do you need help?»

I thought that everything revolved around money, damned 'social-capitalism'!

Later on, I found accommodation in a *posada*; with the few dollars left I could pay for a two-night stay, but what would I do then?

There I met Douglas from Edinburgh, Antoxa from Bilbao and François from Brussels, and I asked them:«I'm going to La Higuera but I don't know where I can withdraw some cash.»

«There are no banks here,» Alex said «But in a couple of months I'll arrive in Cuzco. I can give you some money, one day you'll give it back to me.»

Thank you Alex! We had just met, but had already become best friends!

I hitchhiked to the forest with Antoxa and Douglas, then they stopped at an intersection, while I continued my journey. We had a 'queer' hug in the middle of the forest and promised to meet again, and actually we managed to meet some years later between Edinburgh, Bilbao and Frankfurt.

The vehicles passing by were few, but they all stopped, unlike in Europe. Eventually, at night, I arrived in a village near La Higuera. The truck driver who carried me there said: «Now you should find accommodation; if you go on, you'll meet only figs and snakes. Goodnight, girl! Thank you for the company.»

I bumped into a plain inn and there I saw Juan Carlos, a boy who came from Mexico.

«What are you doing here?» I asked him.

«The same thing that you are doing here, I guess. I'm looking for El Che.»

We decided to continue our journey together; the next day, at dawn, we were ready to explore the forest. We were at two thousand meters above sea level, the path was covered with the dust of the trucks that stopped as soon as we raised the thumb, blessed civilisation!

We often stood for hours, packed like sardines, together with some local farmers, transported on the back of those giant sixteen-wheeled monsters where everything could happen: we ate, slept, talked and danced to the rhythm of samba. In the evening we arrived in La Higuera; we were tired, but did not know where to sleep, therefore we asked some '*Higuereños*' for hospitality.

Manuel hosted us in his home with the warmth of a friend who had been waiting for us for a long time.

«Come on, guys, I'll prepare a warm supper; you can sleep on that straw bed, you won't be cold.»

This was definitely the best hospitality in the place where the legendary Ernesto Che Guevara spent his last days.

«Many nostalgic people often come here and I welcome them in my house, because I feel tenderness for them. I was here when they caught him; the Americans promised to give twenty thousand dollars to those who provided information on El Che: it was a great sum of money, but we did not betray him. A miserable man who lived on the other side of the mountain sold himself for that money and died some years later in misery. If I could turn back time, I'd follow El Che, I'd fight with him; here it is even worse than before.»

Once in the village square, we were surrounded by a big statue of El Che, pictures of El Che, images of El Che and scents of El Che. The next day we went to school, and all the children knew El Che. The mayor allowed us to visit the museum, which was obviously dedicated to El Che. This is the chair where El Che was sitting, this is the bottle from which El Che drank, these are the clothes that El Che was wearing, this is the backpack of El Che.

«We'd like to see the place where El Che was caught. Can you lead us there?»we asked.

«Of course, but it's a one-day walk from here, are you still willing to go there?»

«Yes, this is precisely our purpose» and we started to walk across the forest of El Che.
We had lost sense of time; I did not even know how many days had passed since our journey had begun, then I thought they could not be just weeks, but rather months. I had left Cuzco and then I had moved to Potosì, Buenos Aires, Asunción, Montevideo, Santa Cruz and finally I had gotten lost in the Bolivian forest for some weeks and did not know when I would see a university room again, but I did not care about it. I was wandering aimlessly, enjoying that sacred place where El Che used to live; we were sweating heavily, the ground was hilly, then there was a small river, then another one, some branches obstructed our path and eventually our guide exclaimed: «This is the place where El Che was caught.»
We stood still as if we were in front of a work of art, we reached the place where El Che was wounded and had to return to the valley.
«If we had had a rifle, we would have fought side by side with El Che.» Guided by these illusions, we finally started our journey back home.

Manuel was waiting for us at the door.
«Are you hungry, guys? I have prepared some chicken with baked potatoes.» The following day, we looked for a truck to return to Samaipata, Cochabamba, Santa Cruz.

We remained in silence, since we travelled in the footsteps of El Che.

VII. Manuelita

During my journey between Colombia and Ecuador, I had learnt of Manuelita, the *libertadora* of the 19th century who had waived all the privileges of her social class to fight against the overseas invaders. She had fallen in love with Simón Bolívar, had left her husband in their farmhouse in Quito and, riding a wild and skittish horse, had crossed Latin America to fight against the Spaniards. She took part in the battle of Ayacucho[32]together with Sucre[33]; she was a heroic leader on the battlefield, then she moved to Bogota, Caracas and Quito with Bolívar. At the end of the war, her *libertador* died in her arms in Santa Marta. During some internal power struggles, she was betrayed by her own comrades; she went into exile to Paita, north of Peru, where she died in misery, a victim of the '*olvido*'[34] by many, but not by those who truly loved her.

---

[32]The battle of Ayacucho took place on 9 December 1824 near the homonymous town of Peru, during the Peruvian war of independence and the Spanish-American wars of independence.

[33]Antonio José Francisco de Sucre y Alcalá (Cumaná, 3 February 1795 - Barruecos, 4 June 1830) was a Venezuelan general, politician and patriot, also known as Gran Mariscal de Ayacucho. He was a supporter of Simón Bolívar, thanks to his great military and diplomatic skills; he was one of the protagonists of the Spanish-American wars of independence, during which he became President of Bolivia, Governor of Peru, general of the army of Gran Colombia and commander of the Southern Army. He is regarded as a Father of the Nation and national hero in Ecuador and Bolivia as he led the army which fought for the independence of those countries.

[34]Oblivion.

Legend has it that even Garibaldi visited her. He reached the north of Peru to meet the woman who had fought the greatest battles against the Spanish tyrants and would have deserved to die as a queen, instead of being overwhelmed by the same power against which she had fought in vain.

Along the streets of Bogota, in the middle of Plaza de Armas, near the Botero Museum, I was looking for the house where Manuelita had lived her best years and where she had denounced a betrayal that would have killed Bolivar. I found some inscriptions dedicated to her in the south of Bolivia and in the Amazon jungle, but especially in the city of Quito, where she was born. We do not even know where she was buried, because her body was burnt together with her writings, however her steps still echo along the streets of Ayacucho or Santa Marta. The steps of a woman who gave up everything, except for her dream of love.

VIII. Moscow

Bearing this beautiful image of Latin America in my mind, I had returned to Bologna when I was offered a job in Moscow and I decided to accept, because the Kremlin is to us Marxists what Mecca is for Muslims. The possibility of living near Red Square and visiting the house of Mayakovski, Chekov, Tolstoy and Stanislavski was a real privilege; on the occasion of my interview via Skype, I said that I was willing to accept any condition just to live in the capital of the Russian Empire.

«How many inhabitants are there?» I asked.

«About eighteen million,» they answered.

Not bad, I thought, «Are there any means of public transport in Moscow?»

«Yes, there is the most beautiful and famous subway in the world, but can you read the Cyrillic alphabet?»

«I can only say 'good morning' and 'good evening' in Russian.»

«That's something, the rest will come by itself.»

I took a flight from Bologna to Moscow with a stopover in Prague.

I received a three-month visa to be renewed, and as soon as I arrived there, I felt like I had come to the edge of the world: people did not speak English and did not even try, after all, why should they speak another language? I was

in the heart of the Soviet regime; those guttural sounds began to fill my mind, *dobrui dien, spakonj noc, dobrui viecer, priviet, spassiba.*
At the airport a taxi driver was waiting for me holding a sign with my name written on it; he had to take me to an apartment where I would be welcomed by the coordinator of the language course. I told him ‘good morning’, ‘good evening’ and ‘thank you’, the only three Russian words that I knew; he led me to his car, which looked like an Italian car of the Sixties. It was brown, battered and dirty, the windows had to be rolled down manually and the handle sounded like it was about to crack at any moment. The outskirts of Moscow were more atrocious than those of Lima; smoke came out of some factories and polluted the air, the buildings had neither style nor taste, it looked like the time of Brezhnev instead of the era of Putin.
However, I was enraptured in particular by the wild nature in Moscow: immense forests and lakes among those monstrous concrete buildings. Then we drove through a forest and I began to fear the worst, because the taxi driver started to speak in Russian and I could not understand anything. Outside there were trees and unpaved roads and then, suddenly, a shopping centre and people standing still with a blank expression at the bus stop.
Eventually, I could distinguish the keyword, '*duma*', home, so I realised that we had arrived. The taxi driver stopped in front of a decaying building; I tried to open the door and

almost feared that it would break off the car, a deafening noise ... don't you use any oil in Moscow? A tall, sturdy boy walked towards us: he spoke in Russian with the taxi driver, then turned to me and said, «Hi, my name is Roberto, I hope you enjoyed your journey.»
I felt relieved; that city was disquieting with its immense distances. After all, I had never been to a city with twenty million inhabitants. And, above all, I had never lived there. We brought my luggage into the house, but the worst was yet to come.
The house was a dirty and dusty hovel, springs came out of the mattress, the fridge was full of rotten food; handles fell from the doors; but is this a house? I had already lived in occupied houses, but there the state of abandonment had already turned into decomposition. Roberto did not know what to do and tried to reassure me. He said: «Well, it looks a little shabby, but your colleague will arrive soon and then we'll decide together what to do.»
One hour later, another taxi stopped in front of the house, a tall and nice girl from Venice got out of it; luckily she could speak Russian. As soon as she saw the house, she was not shocked.
«I've seen worse!» she said. «Here, in Moscow, houses are all like this. Let's take a broom and clean it up.»
So this is how we spent our first evening in Moscow.
We threw away eighteen bags full of rotten food from the kitchen; we found a pile of books in another room that

looked like a library; but what did the previous guests do, apart from reading?

We tried to arrange them in boxes and collected the rubbish in the corridor, then there were clothes, coats, shoes, personal objects; what would we do with all that junk?

Five hours later we were worn out due to the jet lag. The neighbours knocked at our door to ask if we needed something and told us that previously an old woman had lived in that house. A *vieja?* And where was she? Nobody knew, so we called it 'The house de la vieja'. Whenever we wanted to laugh, we used to say *¿dónde está la vieja? ¿Dónde se ha ido la vieja?*

The following day, I had to hold an Italian lesson to some Russians, and Elisabetta accompanied me to the school. We walked for twenty minutes to the subway, took the green line and she pointed at the direction, «Oh my God, the school is near Red Square!»

«Yes,» she answered, «You must get off three stops before the Kremlin. At the end of the lesson, you may even walk to Lenin's mausoleum.»

I was utterly amazed: there were just a few stops from my house to the Kremlin.

Once at school, I witnessed a lesson simulation with some Russian students, who were as handsome and kind as any of the students in the world, however I felt like I were in the eastern most corner of the continent: I can't describe this feeling, but I felt in the air somehow.

The course coordinator gave me the lesson timetable; I had a look at it and it seemed perfect.

In Moscow, the working hour was forty-five minutes, so one hour and a half coincided with two working hours, it was great! I received a fixed monthly salary whether I worked or not. Beyond the agreed twenty hours, I was entitled to an overtime payment. We were pushed to work overtime, although it was not mandatory. I felt protected, therefore, at the end of the lessons, I rushed to Red Square, which was always alive and crowded: there were so many races, cultures and things to be seen and discovered.

Suddenly, at a distance, I distinguished a red dot. The Kremlin, Saint Basil's Cathedral, Lenin's mausoleum, The Bolshoi Theatre, the statue of Marx, Pravda, the Duma, Mayakovski's house.

It was all so big and, at the same time, so wonderfully close to me; following the Cyrillic indications, it was impossible to get lost and, even if I had got lost in Moscow, it was what I wanted to do. In the evening, I was very tired; I went home and pushed the springs of my mattress away to avoid getting hurt.

«It's impossible to sleep in this bed,» I said.

«You're telling me! I'm allergic to dust and tonight I couldn't stop coughing; we must find a solution. I cannot stay here under these circumstances.»

The following day, another colleague arrived in our house. Meanwhile, Elisabetta received a new temporary accommodation. My new colleague was Marisa from Lecce.
After having thrown away twenty bags full of rubbish from the house, the rooms seemed to shine, but Marisa was shocked as soon as she saw the house.
«Should I really live in this rubbish?»
«Rubbish? You should have seen it before we cleaned it up! It would have given you a heart attack!»
And she replied: «If it is not cleaned by tomorrow, I'll leave!»
The language school immediately applied to a cleaning company and a Russian woman came to our house to tidy that dirty house; she had agreed to stay there for four hours, but that time was not enough to clean the kitchen.
«And the corridor? The bathroom? My bedroom?»
Marisa screamed. She was right, after all, but given the situation, we rolled up our sleeves, while Marisa made things complicated treating us like scullions. As often as I could, I swept and dusted, but she controlled and said: «It's not clean yet.»
She treated us like her students and I thought to myself: «*Poor students*.»
She was a social climber and we tried to avoid her not to roll out the red carpet in front of her.

Finally, the house was decent; we even got new mattresses, since we ran the risk of going blind with those springs coming out from the mattress; we even got new blankets, because ours were so full of dust that if you sneezed, you were literally overwhelmed by dust.

Eventually, we were accommodated in three apartments: we were eight young teachers of the Moscow language school. It was an extraordinary experience, also because only two of us spoke Russian, therefore we did not want to go out alone and make a fool of ourselves.

We were afraid of getting lost in the subway: who could give us information in that chaos? Everybody spoke Russian and pointed at the Cyrillic writings: the excitement and terror of living in one of the most beautiful and fascinating cities in the world.

Every day I walked with Michela, a colleague of mine, along the streets of the city: the river was there, then there was the Cathedral of Christ the Saviour, which became popular due to Pussy Riot, the craft market, the house of Gorky and Tolstoy, the Lenin library, the Kremlin spires. And then Pravda, the house of the 'war children' of the Spanish refugees during the civil war, the Stanislavski museum, and the Bolshoi theatre with the works of Chekhov and Solženicyn. And the garden of Bulgakov, where 'The Master and Margarita' took place, and the queue before the theatres, and then the Duma again and the high-fashion shops. Yes, there was high fashion: in

Red Square, right in front of Lenin's mausoleum, there was GUM, the former granary of the city and later a shopping centre featuring the most prestigious brands in the world, from Gucci to Vuitton, from Cristian Dior to Chanel.

These were the great contradictions of Moscow, a city which is still anchored to its past from multiple points of view, but, at the same time, looks to the future and competes against the richest men in the world; I have seen many rich people, but those whom I met along the streets of Moscow exceed all the statistical data of the next twenty years of my life. Cars as big as cruise ships and then elegant cafés, restaurants, furs, theatres and high-fashion shops.

The almost infinite reserves of natural gas have reverted the social classes of one of the greatest symbols of communism in the world; it is one of the few countries in the world where education, healthcare and social services are still granted to anyone in spite of Putin and the dismantling of the Soviet system: not the privilege of few people but the right of everybody. Everything is arranged according to the districts: if you need an electrician, a plumber or a painter, you just have to knock at the door of the district office and they send you one for free. This is a common practice for them, while it is amazing for us.

Thus, when we noticed that there was a leak in our kitchen faucet, we had a panic attack and called the school, then

the interpreter said: «There's an office near your house. Knock at the door and ask for a plumber.»
It took the plumber two hours to repair some failed pieces, and when I asked him:«How much is it?»he answered in amazement: «Excuse me, what do you mean?»
«For your work.»
«You owe me nothing, we are paid by the State.»
I was astounded, but he continued.
«What if someone needed a plumber and had no money?»
He was right, but I was just a common inhabitant of Planet Earth, and he sounded like an extra-terrestrial. I was interested in his reflections and asked him:
«So, if you don't have enough money and can't pay the rent, will they evict you?»
«No! Why should they evict you? Here everyone has their home and nobody can take throw them out.»
«And who gives them a house?»
«The State, obviously. Recently things have changed, but in the past, during the communist period, everyone was entitled to a job, a house, a pension and could study the desired subjects; the school assessed the health of the children's teeth and muscles. Evictions never occurred. But now with Putin things are different: some rights have been denied, while others are still granted. What is the situation in Europe? The TV says that you have big houses and big cars, but it seems that you are not so privileged.»

Moving from Europe to Latin America and from Latin America to Russia was a shocking experience.
In Moscow there were also private schools, but they were different from those in Peru. If you do not leave your cage, you cannot become aware of the chains that bind us to our world, therefore travelling is sometimes difficult, because it helps you reappraise your culture and understand that you are small in a big world.
In Moscow, I was particularly struck by Lenin's mausoleum, which I visited on a Sunday in December together with many silent and friendly people. It was snowing, Red Square was covered with white and soft snow, from a distance you could hear the voices of the people passing by, the craftsmen called the tourists; the Russian guards stared into space. Eventually, I saw Lenin's embalmed and ethereal face, with his left hand closed in a fist as a sign of victory.
Once alone in front of him, I felt small and helpless, I even cried; Vladimir Il'ič Ul'janov, a man that I would have gladly understood, embraced, invited to dinner; he looked like he had died just few hours earlier, while in fact he had been staying there for decades.
Then, in December 2011, the elections were called. We witnessed countless meetings of Putin and his opponents, arrests, tortures and the imprisonment of the opponents to the established power. One day, I saw ten kilometres of armoured vehicles, and fifty thousand policemen were sent

by Putin to intimidate the opposers, but the latter protested in front of the cameras from the whole world; women and old and young people shouted from the streets near Red Square and were beaten, but they still protested against a system that was going to enslave them, as happened with the tsars. The policemen were two metres tall and dragged the protesters away like small bundles; the secret police identified the opponents, then those giant men flung them into the armoured vehicles. The brave opponents kept on protesting in front of the curious and scared tourists; if I had been stopped by the policemen, I would have said that I was doing shopping in Red Square, although we had been advised to stay away from the internal affairs of the Soviet state.

As happened with Stalin, the opponents were eliminated; it makes no difference whether it is a communist or imperialist regime.

IX. Cervantes

One day I was called by the Cervantes Institute: they asked me if I could present my book on POUM[35]; we scheduled the event and they offered me an interpreter and a conference room. At the end of the conversation, I was in seventh heaven. I had been studying Stalinism and anti-Stalinism for years, I had watched *Nikolai's case* dozens of times, which was set in the Moscow archives, and I had bumped into Andreu Nin - leader of the party to which also the famous English writer George Orwell had adhered -many times in Barcelona, Cairo, Madrid and Moscow. Like Trotsky[36], he was killed by the Stalinists and his murder dishonoured the left wing; who killed Nin? His murderers were not executed, but we know that the murder was committed upon request of the Stalinists, who wanted to get rid of a man who opposed Stalin, and Stalin did not split hairs.

Walking along the streets of Moscow, I thought of the man who knew Lenin, Zinoviev and Trotsky, took part in

---

[35] Workers' Party of Marxist Unification. The POUM aimed at establishing a large political organisation in Spain able to start a revolutionary process.

[36] Lev Davidovic Trotsky (Janovka, 7 November 1879 – Mexico City, 20 August 1940) was, together with Lenin, one of the greatest Marxists of the 20th century. He dedicated his whole life to the protection of the working class as well as to international socialism.

the party meetings and was not welcomed once back in Spain.
Too close to Trotsky and too far away from Stalin, he escaped to Norway, walking across Europe; then he returned to Catalonia and founded the Workers' Party of Marxist Unification.
When, in May 1937 in Barcelona, the Stalinists took the Telephone exchange managed by the anarchists, the members of the POUM came to the defence of the libertarian movement and Stalin decreed the death of Nin, of the POUM as well as of all the supporters of the party. They were swept up from their homes and the party seats; *La Batalla*, their newspaper, closed, their radio station was confiscated, their army was dissolved and the members of the party were imprisoned. Nin was arrested in Las Ramblas, was kidnapped and tortured. The political instigators of the murder were Togliatti, Longo and Vidali, members of the III International and murderers of Stalin in Spain.
Thus, in the heart of the cruellest power in the world, with a European passport and a published book against the crimes committed by Stalin, I was staring at the house of Mayakovski precisely in front of Lubyanka[37], the most atrocious place of imprisonment and torture in the world.

[37]Lubyanka is the name of a palace in Moscow, which hosted the Soviet and then Russian secret services.

When I arrived at the Cervantes Institute to present my book, the room was crowded: a journalist was waiting for me and the Institute staff were extraordinarily kind to me.
«We are proud of having you here,» they said, «After all, if we don't denounce the crimes of Stalin here in Moscow, then who will do it?»
The director talked about Nin, the POUM and the history of its members, the interpreter translated the *The Nikolai case* short film from Spanish into Russian, then I took the floor, the conference began and Stalin turned in his grave.

X. Lisbon

After the freezing cold of the Far East, I decided to move to the outer point of the continent, to the country of the Carnation revolution which mostly reminded me of South America. There I met Simona, who had left Rome some years earlier to live in Lisbon. She worked as a projectionist, restored old films and organised events at a film library; then she was hit by the crisis and started to paint and sell *azulejos*[38] at the city fairs. An unstable but respectable life, an uncertain but fascinating future.

Whenever I think of Simona, I recall the best years of our life spent under the colonnade of Bologna. I studied politics and she studied dramatic art; our lives led in the open. We celebrated a revolution which is still red, like the colour of our love.

---

[38]Typical ornament of the Portuguese and Spanish architecture consisting of a thin ceramic tile characterised by a glazed and decorated surface.

XI. Sarajevo

I remember a night spent with a girl in Sarajevo. We talked about art and literature, then suddenly she stopped and said:

«They entered our library and burnt our books, the ashes filled our houses, the smell was unbearable My grandmother tried to pick up the pieces of paper that flew in the rooms.

"We must save our culture," she said. It was heart-breaking to see her like that: she did not want to let them humiliate us so much; but why did they do it?»

Her grandmother died shortly after this event and the child grew up during a ten-year war that she still cannot forget.

«You know,» she added «This damned war has taken my youth away. My family was very tight; in spite of the war, we studied, we were afraid of the Serbs, it was absurd. They destroyed our religion and culture; they shot at us from the streets, we saved our lives thanks to a tunnel but we lived like moles for years. They raped our women and left us in anger, misery and desolation. There is nothing to forgive: we can only pretend to forget, because if we remember what they did to us, we won't be able to get out of this blind alley. We are welcoming people, we had one of the largest and most important libraries in the world, we were the small Istanbul and we were proud of our history.

Why did they burn our books? Was it not enough to occupy our houses? They tore our soul apart. No, it was not a war, it was an invasion. The Serbs took our life, our hope, our youth away. I was fifteen years old, and then twenty; who will ever give me back those years lost under the bombs?»

I am sorry, but I cannot imagine your childhood, and in front of any sign of explosion on the walls, I felt ashamed of belonging to a continent that simply looked away, while Mostar and Sarajevo were pitilessly bombed.

The fact that there was a war near us seemed so strange to us; we felt powerless, because we did not know what to do.

«Just think of your friend.»

«Who?»I asked.

«The girl who is travelling with you. She hasn't understood anything about this story; she has come here to take some pictures under the bombs and then go home with a smile on her face. She has been in the bathroom for two hours and she's using the same amount of water that one hundred of us would have used during the war. We were walking in front of the cemetery and she asked:"Who was buried here?"

"My father," I answered.

And she asked again: "When was this church built?"

For her there is no difference between Sarajevo and Chicago.»

I was overwhelmed by shame; then Carla got out of the bathroom and asked:«What time will the housemaid come tomorrow?»
We were speechless. Then she went to the bedroom and came back to us as if something serious had happened.
«The mattress is bigger than the bedstead.»
«Then, what is the problem?» I asked her.
«The problem? I want my bed to be comfortable.»
Fortunately, she did not ask her to fill the holes left by the bombs in the walls with some plaster.
«I apologise for her,» I said, turning to the girl who was hosting us.
«Don't worry, all the tourists who come to Sarajevo behave like that, but you are different; my grandmother used to say that it was better to starve than to die due to ignorance, now can you understand why? I work at the Ministry, I'm fine here, but justice must be served. They did atrocious things to us; don't forget us, please.»

XII. Ceglie

In 2013, in the summer, Maca'n and I had arranged to meet in Apulia, because we wanted to spend some time at the seaside after a long winter under the colonnade of Bologna. We had met some years earlier in the Andes, in the legendary city of Cuzco. She studied Italian, painted on canvas and dreamed of travelling around the world, therefore, after an excursion to the Inca ruins, we decided to visit the south of the world.
We went to the Great Lakes region, to the Chilean Patagonia, and then to Puerto Tombo, Argentina, to watch the penguins, and again to Foz do Iguaçu to admire the wonderful waterfalls; finally, we returned to Chan Chan, Peru, the biggest and most fascinating mud city of the world. We travelled so much that we often stayed home for a few months to recover our strength.

She had arrived in Europe a few months earlier than me; I had stayed in Lima for a longer time, because I loved its alleys, my students and the human warmth that I could perceive everywhere in the city.
In Bologna Maca'n focused on engraving and graphic arts, and began to exhibit her works in the most prestigious galleries in Europe and in the whole world; nobody has ever been able to achieve these great goals in such a short

time. Evidently, the motto saying "Fortune favours the brave" is true.

And so, between a dream of love and a journey across the Alps, we finally met in Apulia.

I had to present my books in Lecce, Alberobello and Ostuni, the city where I was born.

One afternoon we decided to visit Ceglie, an extraordinary melting pot in the Itria valley, twenty kilometres away from the Tyrrhenian and Adriatic coasts. We were walking along its white alleys, when suddenly, in the old square, we saw a billboard attached to a house saying "For sale".

«It's beautiful!» I exclaimed. «Let's call the estate agency and see what it's like inside!»

When the agent opened the door, Maca'n and I were astounded: there were stone booths, bedrooms with closets carved into the wall, windows overlooking the square, and the sea could be seen in the distance.

«Maybe we are doing something crazy, but … what about buying it?»

I needed to settle down in the land where I was born; I owed it to my father, who is buried there, and also to myself, because I really wanted to live in a little white house near the sea. Moreover, I owed it to all the friends of mine who had always supported and believed in me, while my family had taken away what I had the right to enjoy; eventually, I owed to Maca'n, who had always accompanied me and followed my impulsive decisions and passions.

Maca'n looked at me and said:«So are we really going to buy this house?»
«Yes, obviously! You don't need to ask that!»
«But we don't have the money for furniture.»
Then Marta came into play. «I have saved some money. If you agree, we may use it.»
Obviously, we agreed, so we completed the house purchase.

The Itria valley is beautiful, a melting pot of people, seas and worlds; the rebels are beautiful, now and forever, from Madrid to Chicago, from Ceglie to London, from Prague to Sarajevo.
Now the house is there, with its imposing structure, for us and for everybody: it looks at us with a sly smile, waiting to be filled.

From a distance, I saw Maca'n performing a pirouette.
«It's wonderful!" she said, «Ceglie is wonderful!»
And she was right: Ceglie is really wonderful.

INDEX

INDEX

Printed in October 2018
by Andersen S.p.A.
for Youcanprint *Self-Publishing*